FEATHER BOY

BOY

a novel by

Nicky Singer

a dell yearling book

Published by
Dell Yearling
an imprint of
Random House Children's Books
a division of Random House, Inc.
New York

First published in Great Britain by Collins,
a division of HarperCollins Publishers, in 2002

Visit us on the Web! www.randomhouse.com/kids

Educators and librarians, for a variety of teaching tools, visit us at www.randomhouse.com/teachers

ISBN: 0-440-41858-5

Reprinted by arrangement with Delacorte Press

Printed in the United States of America

November 2003

10 9 8 7 6 5 4 3 2 1

OPM

For Roland
—inspiration, accomplice, son—
with my love

PART ONE

Chance House

1

It all began when Catherine came to talk about the Elders' Project. Of course that's not what Catherine would say. She'd say it began in a time that is yesterday and tomorrow and eternally present. But then Catherine's a storyteller. I'm not a storyteller. I'm just the guy it happened to.

Anyway, there we all were in that dead time just after lunch, a little pale sunlight trying to push its way into Class 7R. Miss Raynham had set out a chair for Catherine and patted its seat to make her sit down. She'd said "Ahem" and begun to scratch her head.

None of us likes it when Miss Raynham scratches her head. Her thin gray hair barely covers her very white scalp. The merest touch of a fingernail on that creepy skull showers her shoulders with dandruff. Niker says if she ever loses her job as a teacher she could earn a living making snowdrifts for the movies. When I told my mum that story (and I made the story mainly about Niker) Mum said: "That's nothing." Apparently, when she was at school, they had a teacher called Miss Cathart, who used to spit down the sleeves of her cardigan. Miss Cathart's cardigans, Mum says, were the crocheted sort. Loosely knitted. With holes in. So the spit ran out.

This is the problem with stories. They run on. So—to begin again: Miss Raynham says: "Ahem." And then. "This is Catherine. Catherine erm . . ."

"Deneuve," says Niker.

"Of Aragon," says Derek.

"Parr," says Weasel.

You can see we've been learning about Henry VIII. Well, everyone but Niker has.

"Class," says Miss Raynham, and she shifts down-wind—fast. She's big, Miss Raynham, corpulent, a blob on legs. But she moves like a spider. One minute she's standing at the front of the class with a smile and a piece of chalk and the next thing you know, she's zig-zagged to your desk and the chalk is in your neck. Or Niker's neck in this case.

4

"Catherine Fenn," continues Miss Raynham without a pause, "has come to speak to us about the Elders' Project. Catherine?"

Attention transfers at once to the front of the class. Catherine is youngish, in her twenties probably, little, dark, and she seems at rather a loss. Her long hair is piled up on her head and held in place with a moon and stars clip. Only the clip isn't doing a very good job and most of the hair is making a bid for freedom down Catherine's back. She's wearing those brightly colored clothes that look like you've dipped them at random in three different vats of dye and—as yet—she hasn't said anything.

"Catherine," repeats Miss Raynham with that scratch and that edgy irritation we all know so well.

"Hello," says Catherine at last.

"Hello, Catherine," says the class.

She shifts position, as though she's Goldilocks and she can't get comfortable in Mummy Bear's chair. "Thank you for letting me be here."

"Oh boy," says Niker, and then seems to choke. Could be the chalk at his throat.

"I . . . ," begins Catherine, but Miss Raynham's patience is at an end. She strides to the front of the class.

"Catherine is a storyteller. We're very fortunate to have her on loan from Icarus, an arts organization working with people in the community. Catherine is going to lead a project between children from this class and the residents of the Mayfield Rest Home."

"Is that the barmy bin?" asks Weasel.

"No, Wesley, it is not the barmy bin. And it is partly to counter such ignorant attitudes about the senior members of our society that this project is being undertaken. Now, since we apparently need to return to basics, can anyone tell me what a rest home is?"

Niker's hand goes up. "It's a vegetable shop," he says.

"Jonathan Niker. Explain yourself."

"Well, my aunt Maisie was there and she was a vegetable."

"In a time that was yesterday and tomorrow and eternally present," says Catherine suddenly, "there lived a prince who had been silent for as long as anyone could remember." Her voice is so low and urgent that even Niker doesn't say "Fat chance." "And," Catherine continues, "his mother the Queen was heartbroken at her son's muteness and the King heartbroken at his wife's grief. So it was that, on the Prince's eighteenth birthday, the King issued a proclamation saying that any man or woman who could make the Prince speak would receive the richest reward in the kingdom. However, the penalty for those who tried and failed would be instant death."

"Cool," says Weasel.

"They tell nursery stories in the nursery," says Niker, twirling the sharp point of a pencil in the palm of his hand.

"Does that mean," Catherine asks, faster than Miss Raynham, "you think this class is too grown up for such tales?"

"Yes," says Niker. "Except"—he scans his fellow pupils—"maybe Norbert there."

Norbert is the class squit. He's thin and gangly, his arms and legs like white string loosely knotted at the elbows and knees. His head is too big for his body, and where other people have hair, he has this yellow, fluffy duck's down. His eyes are blue, though it's difficult to see that through the thick glass of his spectacles. If you take his specs off him, and people do, he looks startled. Naked. His real name isn't Norbert, it's Robert. Robert Nobel. But I don't think anyone's ever called him that. In kindergarten, when his hair was even more yellow than it is now, they called him Chick or Chickie. Even Mrs. Morgan. But since Niker arrived in school, it's been Norbert. Norbert No-Bel. Norbert No-Bells-at-All. Norbert No-Brain. Norbert No-Bottle. I don't suppose Johnny Niker, who has curly dark hair, green eyes and a fluid, athletic body, has ever imagined what it would be like to look out at the world through Norbert

No-Bottle's spectacles. But I have. Because I am Norbert No-Bottle.

"Personally," says Catherine, "I think one never grows out of fairy tales. I think fairy tales contain all of the ways we sort experience, good and bad. In fact, I think stories are the most important form of communication we as human beings have."

"Ahem," says Miss Raynham.

"What do you think, Jonathan?"

"Johnny," says Niker.

"I don't think Johnny is a human being," says Weasel.

"Right," says Miss Raynham. "That is quite sufficient, thank you. The purpose of the Elders' Project is, as Catherine will explain at greater length, to share experiences between young and old. And to learn something. Manners perhaps."

It's Norbert No-Bottle that hurts the most. No-Bottle. Where does that phrase come from? From the soccer bleachers, I think. From when fans smash bottles and jab the broken glass in other fans' faces. Have you got the "bottle" to do that? More to the point, would you want to? Niker might. But maybe I'm being unfair because, of course, Niker didn't use broken glass. He used a grape. That's when he started using the name. After the Grape Incident. Maybe I'll tell that story later. Right now I can't even say the word "grape" without feeling sick. And I still get queasy going down the aisles at Sainsbury's supermarket, just in case I encounter any big, fat, green grapes.

"We're going to be telling stories," says Catherine. "About our lives and those of the Elders. We might look at their childhood experiences compared with yours. Or their wisdoms and yours. And then we're going to try to make a piece of work that records the things we find out."

"What sort of work?" asks Kate.

"I'm not entirely sure yet. Probably some sort of large picture, or pictures, a collage perhaps of writings, paintings, photos, mementoes. I think we should be looking at two pieces of work. One which might eventually hang in the school and one in the home."

"Groovy," says Weasel.

"Naturally," says Miss Raynham, "not everyone will be able to take part in the project. Working space at Mayfield limits the numbers we can reasonably send."

"So we'll be going to the home?" asks Derek.

"Yes. On Wednesday afternoons. For the next four or five weeks. So"–Miss Raynham's chin juts challengingly forward–"I'm looking for about ten volunteers."

That's when people look at Niker. Nothing

obvious, just a quick glance, a sidelong peek. Is this project going to be for the Cool Gang or the Class Duffers? Is it a good thing or a bad? Will Niker give it his seal of approval? He sits there (I'm looking too, of course) like some Roman emperor, imperious, disdainful, savoring the lengthening moments during which the rest of us wait to know whether the project lives or dies.

My hand goes up.

"Thank you, Robert. Robert Nobel." She writes my name on a list.

Niker scowls furiously. I have jumped the gun. Now no one else will volunteer, because the class pariah is going. This is power of a sort I suppose, to be able to make something untouchable by touching it. In any case there are no more hands.

"Come on, come on." Miss Raynham is embarrassed, agitated. "Miss Finch will be accompanying the Mayfield group. The rest of you"—she glares—"will be remaining here with me."

Liz Finch, our student teacher, is bland, harmless and has no known habits. So, normally, this would be a good ploy. But everyone knows that Wednesday afternoon is actually PE (with Mr. Burke) and double art (with Mrs. Simpson), which is why people continue to roll scraps of paper between fingers and thumb and stare out of windows.

"If there are no more volunteers, I shall be forced to choose."

"Many brave men and women," says Catherine, "tried to make the young Prince speak. And as many were beheaded. The King and Queen had all but given up their quest when, from the woods nearby, came one last adventurer. . . ."

Kate's hand goes up. I might be imagining it but I think I hear the grind of Niker's teeth. Of all the people he'd want not to go, she'd be top of the list. Not that I think she's challenging him, it's just that the project obviously intrigues her and, unlike some other people in the class, Kate has a mind of her own. That's why I like her. I'd like to say she likes me back. But actually I don't think she's any more conscious of me than she might be of a wood louse. Niker she has noticed, not least because he says "Stylish" every time she passes. I keep waiting for her to wither him with some remark. But she doesn't. Sometimes, she even smiles.

"Kate Barber," notes Miss Raynham. "Thank you."

Kate's friend Lucy then puts her hand up and the spell seems to break. Oliver, Tom and Mai and a couple of others volunteer. Only Derek continues to haver.

"Right," says Miss Raynham, doing a quick count-up. "I make that eight. So, if we add in young Wesley

Parr and Mr. Niker here, I think we have a full complement."

So that's how, the following Wednesday, I find myself at the Mayfield Rest Home, starting a project that's going to change my life forever.

2

The Mayfield lounge is like a dentist's waiting room: green chairs lined up against the walls and that dull, limbo feeling of time having moved elsewhere. On top of the television set in the far corner is a crochet mat and on the windowsill are some fake flowers in white plastic pots. We arrive after lunch and the residents are already seated. Some are in the green chairs, perched on plastic cushions, others have brightly colored patchwork blankets tucked around their knees, and a walking stick or walker nearby. Some are sunk in wheelchairs.

Their hush seems to fall on us as we enter the room. A disconsolate, decrepit hush. And all of a sudden the ten of us are trying to huddle behind Catherine as though we're embarrassed for being so full of life. Some of the residents peer at us, others ignore us, or maybe they just don't see us. Niker shifts from foot to foot. I concentrate on the floor. The carpet is gold and swirly. If Miss Raynham were here she'd take charge, but Miss Raynham is not here. As we wait—and wait—for Catherine to do something, a wheelchair suddenly shrieks: "I think I'm in the wrong place!"

"Join the club," says Niker.

"Now, now," says Matron. "Mavis."

Mavis is a chicken in a dress. At once bony and fleshy, her plucked yellow skin springs with coarse hair. At some stage her neck must have been chopped out and her head stuck straight back onto her shoulders.

"What's going on?" she asks.

"It's the Project," says Matron, enunciating loudly and clearly as though talking to a foreigner or an imbecile, "with the children."

"Oh," says Mavis. "When's tea?"

"Hello," says Catherine, finally arriving at the television set, the room's focal point. Then she adds, in her rather faltering way, "I'm Catherine."

"Two of my family died in this place," says Mavis.

"No, they didn't," says Matron briskly. "Now, children, why don't you all sit down?"

Gratefully we sit. The residents shuffle and cough and peer.

"Hello," says a relatively normal and fit-looking man, leaning down toward me. "Who's this then?"

"Robert," I whisper.

"Oh aye," he says. "What yer doing here, Robert?"

Catherine begins to explain. Because she's standing and we're all sitting, she's just about big enough to command attention. She talks briefly about the project and then suggests we work in pairs.

"Just space yourselves out a bit," she tells the class, "that's right, into a ring. Now, introduce yourself to whoever you're closest to. That person will be your main partner. Though, of course, we'll all be sharing ideas later on."

As chance would have it, I'm still closest to Mr. Relatively Normal. Niker, however, is sitting at Mavis's feet.

"I'm Robert," I repeat quickly, to establish my claim.

"So yer said," he replies. "I'm Albert. Robert and Albert. Bert and Bert. Do they call you Bert?"

"No."

"Oh aye," Albert says.

There's a pause and then he says, "I were a ladies'

man. Once." And he sighs. The sigh is sad and re-signed but it's only a moment before he leans down and smiles at me. "Eh up, lad."

There's something tender in his look, not a tender-ness for me of course, just something misty about his past, and in that moment I indulge a few warm thoughts of my own about my grandfather, Grandpa Cutting, who used to call me lad and take me boating before he died of a heart attack hanging a garage door. And I'm just thinking maybe Albert will be all right and perhaps the Nobel luck is going to change when a voice chisels through the room:

"I don't want this one."

Everyone turns to the speaker. She is tall (even seated), white-haired, ramrod-backed, and her per-fectly still right index finger is pointing down at Kate.

"Well," flusters Liz Finch, the student teacher, who, up until this point, might have been a sheet of wallpaper, "perhaps you'd like to swap with Kate, Lucy. Lucy?"

Lucy isn't moving.

"Lucy?"

"No," says Ramrod. "I don't want a girl." The index finger lifts, it moves. "I want a boy. In fact"—the finger stops midswing—"I want him." She's pointing at me.

Now, you know those team games where there are two captains and they each pick someone to be on their side, turn after turn, until there's only one person left? And no matter whether there are ten or twenty players that last person is always the same? The one who is never chosen, whatever the game? Well, that person's me.

"Robert, isn't it?" says Catherine.

And all the times I've prayed, I've pleaded, I've begged to be chosen and God's ignored me? And now—

"Norbert," says Niker. "She wants Norbert!"

Niker's jeering does not deter Ramrod. She beckons me and I just know I'm going to have to go.

"Norbert," repeats Albert, meditatively.

Kate is already halfway across the room. I stand up.

"Sorry," I say as we pass like substituted soccer players at the edge of the field.

"You're joking," she says.

A moment later I'm face to face with Ramrod. Close to, she looks surprisingly frail. Her body so thin and bloodless, she must, I think, be sitting upright by force of will alone.

"I'm Robert," I say, extending a polite hand.

"Edith," she replies, ignoring the hand. "Edith Sorrel."

My arm drops uselessly and me with it. I'm back on the floor.

Then, like the cavalry, the tea trolley arrives. It comes with clink and clatter and shout and "Thank God" from Albert. Catherine, obviously taken aback that tea can be so early, suggests we all use the time to get "better acquainted." We know what this means because Liz Finch briefed us on the bus.

"Remember your Elder may be deaf," she said. "Just ask short, simple questions. Do you have children? Grandchildren? A husband, wife? What job did you used to do? And speak up."

"Do you have children?" I ask Edith Sorrel.

"No."

I pause, leave a gap. This is the art of conversation, you know. You say something. They say something. You say something.

Edith says nothing.

"A husband?" I inquire hopefully.

"No."

Another pause. Longer this time. I watch the trolley coming, so very slowly round toward us.

"Looking forward to tea?"

"No."

The trolley passes us. The staff obviously know that Edith does not take tea, she does not take biscuits. The biscuits are those oblong ones which say "Nice" on them and are covered in sugar. I watch them go Weasel's way.

"Did you have a job?"

Behind me I can hear Kate's Albert. He had a job. He worked "in sawmills" and then "on the building," he got paid sixpence a day.

"How much is sixpence?" asks Kate.

"Eh?" says Albert.

"Sixpence—how much was it worth?"

"Three loaves of bread, that's what sixpence were."

"No," says Edith Sorrel. "I did not have a job. Young women were not encouraged to have jobs."

And then I think she's not really trying and it's not fair and anyhow I'm cross about the biscuits, so I say: "Any special reason why you didn't want a girl?"

"No."

"OK. Any special reason for wanting me?"

She stares at me. Under her gaze, I feel quite transparent. As though she's looking straight through me and out the other side.

"I mean me," I persist, "me rather than any other boy?"

"No," says Edith Sorrel.

"Well," says Catherine, as the tea trolley finally beats a retreat, "I'd like to tell you all a story."

"Oh aye," says Albert.

Edith Sorrel clasps her hands in her lap. And I have this weird sensation that she's holding herself, trying to comfort herself.

"It's about a silent prince and the young woman who wants to free him from the curse that has rendered him mute. The Prince's mother and father, the King and Queen, have promised the riches of their kingdom to anyone who can make the young man speak. But for those who try and fail, the penalty is to be instant death."

"Is it *Neighbours?*" asks Mavis.

"You daft brush," says Albert.

"Well, the young woman knew it would take more than skill or cunning or luck to make the Prince speak, for many had gone before her and as many had lost their lives. So the young woman took herself into the forest where her grandparents lived. And as they sat around the cottage after supper, she told them of her plan.

"'Oh, my beloved,' cried her grandmother, 'you know not what you ask.'

"'Indeed I do, Grandmother,' said the girl. 'And that is why I'm here. I have come to listen and to learn. For you and Grandfather have lived long in the forest and understand how it is that night turns into day and winter into spring. And if this were not enough, you have lived long in each other's hearts and so understand the dark and light of love, and if this were not enough you have read many books and told many stories and so know what makes a beginning and what an end. I beg you, Grandparents, share what you can with me, for I am eager to know what you know and to carry your wisdom to the Prince.'"

"Nurse," cries Mavis. "Shut the curtains!"

"I've nearly finished now," says Catherine, gently. "If you want to sleep. But you see, the grandparents did tell the girl their wisdom. All night long they spoke and she listened. And I was hoping we could do something similar here."

"What?" says Albert.

"She wants you to tell the children your secrets," shouts Matron.

"No, I won't indeed. They'd be shocked."

"Not secrets," says Catherine. "Wisdoms. Things you've learned over the years."

"Not to be nosey," says Weasel's Elder. "That's what. Mind your own business. That's what. Little piggies have big ears. That's what."

"Well, that's a start," says Catherine.

"That's what," says Weasel emphatically.

"Wesley . . . ," says Miss Finch.

"I'm just repeating the wisdom," says Weasel. "Learning from Dulcie here. That right, Dulcie?"

"Cheeky little blighter," says Dulcie.

"Anything you'd share with me," I say to Edith Sorrel, "if I was going to be beheaded tomorrow?"

"No."

I put my finger to my throat and make the sound of ripping flesh. "That's me gone then."

"What?" For the first time she seems caught off-guard.

"Dead," I repeat. "I'm dead. Just twelve years old and dead. D.E.A.D. Dead. Finished. Kaput. Head on the carpet."

"Stop it," says Edith Sorrel. "Stop it at once."

"Can't stop it. Sorry, without the Wisdom, I'm a goner. Didn't Catherine say? Just one or two old forest truths and I'll be OK. You can save me. You do want to save me, don't you?"

She gives me that stare. "Of course. I'd give my life to save you. You know that."

"Oh. Right. Great. Well, you've got to tell me something important then."

"What?"

"I don't know! You're supposed to be telling me. Whatever the most important thing in your life is. Was. Whatever."

"Top-Floor Flat. Chance House, twenty-six St. Albans."

"What?"

"You can go there. Walk. It's not far."

Geography has never exactly been my strong point but I'd say St. Albans has to be two and a half hours' drive from here. So maybe Niker's right about the vegetable shop after all.

"Sure," I say. "I'll go right after school."

"You're such a good boy," she says, and then she reaches up toward my head and gives me this little dry, tender tap. "Beautiful," she murmurs, hand in my hair, "beautiful."

I pull away. "It's horrid," I say, "my hair." And I tell her how they used to call me Chickie.

"I don't see Chickie," she says, and then: "Pass me my bag."

Jammed down the side of the seat is one of those triangular witches' bags, faded black leather with a large gold clasp. I extract it and hand it to her as instructed. From the musty interior she draws out a mirror in a suede case.

"Now." She wipes the surface with the back of her liver-spotted hand. "What do you see?"

She holds the mirror up to her own face. And this is what I see: A spooky old bat with snow-white hair, weird black eyebrows and about a million wrinkles.

"Come on," she urges, "come on."

"I just see a lady."

"No, you don't."

"Well an old . . . erm, an elderly lady then."

"Liar," she says. "Tell me what you see."

But I can't.

So she says, "You see an old hag. A wrinkled old hag. Yes?"

"Maybe."

"So do I." She puts away the mirror. "It always surprises me. You see, I expect to see the girl I was at twenty. With skin and hair like yours. And yet whenever I look—there's the old hag." She laughs quietly.

"Right."

"So you'll go to Chance House for me?"

I'm not sure where the "so" comes from in this. There doesn't seem any "so" about it. But I nod like the sad case I am.

"Good. Thank you."

"Everything OK?" asks Catherine, coming by.

"Oh yeah. Great."

"Good." She moves on but not before Albert bursts into song:

" 'Run rabbit, run rabbit, run run run.' "

"Stop it," says Edith Sorrel. "Stop that at once!"

" 'Don't be afraid of the farmer's gun!' " squawks up Mavis.

"Right on," says Niker.

" 'He'll get by . . . ,' " continues Albert in a gravelly lilt, " 'without a rabbit pie . . .' "

"Stop the singing," says Edith. "Don't sing. I asked you to stop."

"Ole misery guts," mutters Albert.

" 'Run,' " Niker encourages the Chicken, " 'run rabbit . . .' "

Edith draws herself to her feet. She is tall. She

reaches for her stick. For one insane moment I think she intends to hit someone. But of course she only means to walk away.

" 'Run,' " sings Albert jovially to her stiff, retreating back, " 'rabbit, run, run, run.' "

I follow Edith into the corridor. Each stride looks painful.

"Can I help?"

"No," she says. "No. Go away. Leave me alone."

"Don't mind her," says Matron. "She doesn't mean anything by it."

But as Edith shuts the door of her room, I have this horrible feeling that she does mean something by it. All of it.

3

I don't go to Chance House. Not right after school anyway. But I find myself wanting to go. The whole walk home to Grantley Street I keep thinking, "I ought to be going to Chance House. Why aren't I going to Chance House?" And it's not just because I told some batty old woman that I would go, it's because I feel, about as powerfully as I've ever felt about anything, that the house is standing somewhere close, waiting for me. Maybe being batty is catching.

Grantley Street is a thin strip of houses, wedged between two roads. Our front door opens straight onto the pavement of Grantley and our rear patio onto the Lane, which is lucky considering it could open onto the Dog Leg. The Dog Leg can be scary. More about that later.

Our back gate is a nine-foot barricade of wood with a deranged row of nails banged in along the top. It's about two years since Mum made with the hammer, so the points are a bit rusty now. I perform complicated maneuvers with the gate lock, the bolts and chain and then, once inside, remove a loose brick from the garden wall to get at the house keys. A moment later I'm letting myself into the kitchen.

"I can see you," I announce in a loud voice.

I wish I could stop doing this. I'm not quite sure who I'm expecting to find in our kitchen. Niker. A burglar. Dad. But it's part of the routine now, a habit, a mantra. Saying it protects me, gives me one up on Whoever's There. Proves I can't be startled, taken advantage of. Trouble is, I have to do it in every room in the house.

"I can see you!" I yell into the sitting room. Then I thunder upstairs and repeat myself in Mum's bedroom, in mine and finally in the bathroom. This little quirk started about three years ago, when Dad left and Mum took the extra shifts at the hospital. "No choice, now," Mum said. The good news is I don't do the cupboards anymore. I used to shout into the pantry,

Mum's wardrobe and the airing cupboard. This has to be progress.

Of course, I don't yell if Mum's home. Well, I did once, blasted into the kitchen shrieking, "I can see you!" at the top of my voice. Mum was sitting at the kitchen table drinking a cup of coffee.

"That's lucky," she said, "or you'd need new glasses."

They call it obsessive-compulsive behavior. Or compulsive-obsessive or Chance House Bonkers or something. People do it with hand-washing. I read that in the newspapers. They wash their hands again and again and again, four times, six times, twenty times. Then as soon as their hands are dry, it's back to the basin again, wash, wash, wash. Washing until they bleed. By comparison I have to be a mild case. Almost normal in fact. Norbert Normal.

Anyhow. I'm in the house. I'd like to tell you that I get a chocolate biscuit and then go straight on to the computer. Well, I do get the biscuit but then I go upstairs to paint my models. Niker, when he came round, called me a Saddo. I didn't tell him we don't have a computer because of the money. I told him I like painting model soldiers. Which, as it happens, I do. That was a little while after the Grape Incident. Which took place in the Dog Leg. Anyway, I didn't tell Mum anything about anything. But she's not stupid. She'd watched me avoiding the Dog Leg, even though it's the quickest way to school. And one afternoon she asked:

"Is someone on your back?"

"No."

"Someone bullying you?"

"No."

"Do you want to invite anyone home for tea?"

"No!"

"If someone's on your back," she said, "you can always try to make a friend of them. Ask their advice. Get them to help you with something. Invite them home. It sometimes helps."

"Right."

How come grown-ups are always so smart about your life, but not quite so smart about their own? Yell, scream, yell, smash. That was Dad out on the landing. Dad and Mum and the Imari dish. Mum's favorite dish. The one she kept the rose petals in. Smashed against the wall. Well, I don't know if it was the wall, because I wasn't exactly out on the landing taking a look. I was in my room with the door firmly closed. Tell the truth, I didn't really want to look. I could hear plenty enough. Anyhow, I didn't notice Mum trying to make Dad into a friend the next morning.

So what happens? Niker comes home. I didn't think for a moment he'd accept the invitation. In fact, it took me three weeks to pluck up the courage to ask him, and even then I had to write the time and date down and pass it to him like some secret note. I thought he'd laugh. But he just looked at me and said: "Yeah. Why not." Of course Mum had planned to be there, but she hadn't reckoned on a juggernaut jack-knifing on the A23 and plowing into six other vehicles. Like every other member of a nursing staff in Sussex, she was called into Accident and Emergency. So when we got home there was a note on the table and a lasagna in the oven. Niker doesn't like lasagna.

"No computer and no food," said Niker. "On the other hand—no parents."

I had never intended to show Niker the lead soldiers—the ones that were my father's when he was a child. Dad had bought them in Willie Sureen, Sloane Street, with his own pocket money on one of the rare occasions he'd accompanied my grandfather on business to London. No more than half a thumb high, each man is intricately cast, from the sharp tip of his spear to the insignia on his tricorn or the buttons on his spats. Highlanders of the '45 rebellion who died at Culloden, French officers who fought against Wolfe in Canada in the Seven Years War, a single Grenadier guard on his knees with a bayonet, a little drummer boy. Each delicately painted in Humbrol enamel, every silver belt buckle, cross-gartered stocking, black

sporran tassel executed perfectly, every soldier a trib-
ute to the skill of my father, who has such large, un-
gainly hands.

No, I never meant to show Niker these soldiers,
which I keep wrapped in tissue paper in the Huntley
& Palmer Superior Reading Biscuits tin in which Dad
presented them to me on my eighth birthday. I intended to show him the small, less detailed plastic
models, also my father's, from the American War of
Independence. Cavalry, artillery, foot soldiers, painted
more sporadically by Dad, and left in their gray or
blue plastic for me to finish. And painstakingly, with
my sable brushes and thinners, I have been finishing
them. The rifles of these soldiers are flexible, durable,
whereas the smallest, most accidental, tweak can snap
the sword of one of the lead soldiers.

So there they were that day, the plastic models, on
my desk. The horses, the riders, the gun carriages, the
infantry and even one or two odd cowboys, a belly-
scuttling Indian, a First World War soldier, tidbits to
entice. And the paint of course. And the brushes. I
knew it was a risk. But that's what I was doing—risking.

Niker scanned my room. "What's in that tin?"

The Huntley & Palmer tin. Had I been looking?
How could he possibly have known? Why hadn't I
hidden it, stashed it under the bed, secreted it in
Mum's room?

"What tin?"

"This tin."

I feel cold even now when I think of him opening it. His hands on the stiff, slightly rusty lid. Him pulling and peering and me just standing there. The tissue was discolored, brittle.

"What have we here, Norbert?"

He drew out a Highlander, red jacket, green kilt, tam-o'-shanter, a running man, heels kicking, thin bladed bayonet to the fore.

"Jeez," said Niker, looking at the exquisitely painted crisscross leg garters, "did you do this?"

"No, my dad."

"It's good." And he put the soldier down, turned it gently this way and that, admired it. "Very good."

He unwrapped and looked at every soldier in the same way, taking time and care, asking me what I knew about the uniforms.

Two hours later Mum found us both sitting at my desk, paintbrushes in hand. The lasagna, which I'd forgotten to turn down, was burnt, but there were fifteen chestnut horses with black bridles, blue saddlecloths and fifteen horse stands. Niker had painted mud and grass on his stands. And also flowers.

Mum's smile was so broad. But premature. Nothing changed at school. In fact it remained so much the same, I sometimes think that Niker never came to my house at all. But then I sometimes think that my father, with those heavy hands, could never have painted the Highlanders. And he did.

So here I am again, sitting at my desk with the smell of turpentine about me and thinking about Niker because it's preferable to thinking about what I'm actually thinking about. Which is Chance House.

You know how it is when there's something niggling you, and you do your best to refuse it, chain it up in some dark and faraway place, only to have it come yap yap yapping back at you like some demented dog? Well, yap yap yap, here it comes again. Chance House.

"You can go there. Walk. It's not far."

I'm really not painting. I'm just waving a brush about. So I might as well—yap yap—go downstairs and get Mum's road atlas. This is how she finds me, crouching over England with a piece of string in my hands.

"Geography prep?" she asks, practical as ever.

"Yap."

"What is it?"

"Distance in miles from here to St. Albans. How far do you reckon, Mum?"

"You're the one with the string."

"Right. Fine. Ninety miles. Would it be ninety miles?"

"Sounds about right."

"Could we go there?"

"Why?"

Good question.

"Day out?"

She sits down, kicks off her shoes and puts her feet up on a little pouffe.

"Bit far for a day out," she says. My mum is a small person, with a small face and a little puff of blond hair. She looks exhausted.

"Can I get you a cup of tea?"

"God bless you, Robert."

It's only teabag tea but, the way she takes it, it could be water in a desert.

"I'd really like to go to St. Albans. In fact, I think I have to go to St. Albans."

She shuts her eyes.

"Do you think we could?"

"Mmm." She's asleep. I lift the teacup from her lap. Where her skirt has ridden up I can see blood throbbing in her varicose vein.

In the kitchen I make myself a sandwich and then I return to my desk.

"It's really not far," yaps Edith Sorrel.

That's when I decide to set the dream alarm. It's not an exact science but it sometimes works for me. All I have to do is think about whatever it is that's bothering me and then set the alarm for 3 A.M. I've tried many different times of night but all my best results have come from 3 A.M. Too early in the night and my dreams don't really seem to have got going, too near the morning and they seem to be petering out. At 3 A.M., I'm normally in the middle of some seething epic. As soon as the alarm goes, I start scribbling. I write down everything I can remember in my dream diary. Even the stupid and inconsequential stuff. Mainly that, actually. I note all the colors, the people, the buildings, the looks, the feelings. But I don't try to make sense of anything. In any case there often isn't much sense to be made. But in the morning it's different. Once or twice I've woken with some completely crystalline idea about a problem. An idea which often bears no relation to whatever I scribbled down in the night, but it's still there like some perfect jewel on my pillow. Of course, it's not always like that. Much more often I have to go back to the diary, reading and rereading until something jumps out at me—a word, a color, a phrase, a clue. Something to work with. Naturally, I always hope for the jewel. But somehow I can't see that happening with Chance House.

Once I've decided to use the dream alarm, the evening normally passes mournfully slowly. But not tonight. It only seems a moment before I'm in bed. Then it's just a matter of going through the ritual. I lie on my back, close my eyes and relax my body, starting with my feet. When all my limbs are so heavy that the mattress seems dented with them, I turn to my mind. This is when it can get tricky. I think about the problem—in this case Chance House—but I try not to direct my thoughts. It works better if I can keep everything loose and unfocused. If images come, and they do, I attempt to follow them, but not to pursue them, so they can choose their own way. It normally takes a while for the vague, meandering flow to begin. But Chance House conjures itself at once, arriving exact and massive in my imagination. It's a huge edifice of dirty cream brick. Wide concrete steps lead to a forbidding door. The door handle is a twisted ring of metal, fashioned like a rope. I imagine myself walking up the steps, grasping the handle in both hands and passing boldly into Edith's past and my future. But that's not what happens. I do walk up the steps. But the moment I touch the door, there are a flash and a bang and the house disappears. Or that's what I believe at first. A little while later, as I stand in the dark, it occurs to me that maybe I have disappeared.

4

Next thing I'm aware of is Mum shaking me by the shoulders.

"Robert," she says gently.

At once I'm in action mode, it can't be more than three seconds before I'm bolt upright, pencil in hand.

"Room," I write in my dream diary. "Small, cozy, warm, not unlike my bedroom."

"Robert?"

"People: me, Mum. Atmosphere: everyday, normal. Colors: pale but bright, morning colors."

Mum gets up and opens the curtains. It is bright. In fact, it is morning.

I grab for my clock, focus. Focus again.

"You set the alarm for three A.M.," says Mum. "You silly chump." She smiles, touches me lightly on the head.

"What!"

"Lucky I noticed, eh?" says my mother.

I fall backward onto the bed. She reset the alarm. She reset the alarm! I don't believe it. I pull the duvet over my head.

"Come on now," she says, "seven-thirty. Chop chop."

She leaves.

I wail, I moan, I thump the mattress. Then I get dressed.

"I'm on lates," says Mum over breakfast. "Do you want me to walk you to school?"

"No," I say. "No, thanks." Niker says only girls and wusses are walked to school.

Mum notes what I eat (one slice of toast with strawberry jam), what I drink (nothing), and then she follows me to the bathroom and fiddles about while I clean my teeth. She watches me put my library book and soccer cleats in my schoolbag and then I watch her as she takes them out again. She puts the cleats, which are mud-free, in a plastic bag, examines the library book, remarks, "Haven't you read this before?" and then replaces both items in the bag. After which she checks the time.

"You don't have to go yet," she says.

It's twenty to nine. The journey to school—via the Dog Leg—is about five minutes. "I like being early," I say. "I get to use the computers." Actually Mr. Biddulph doesn't get in till nine-thirty and the computer room is locked like Fort Knox. But Mum doesn't know that.

"I'll get you a computer one day," she says. "I'll save up."

"I didn't mean that."

"I know you didn't, love."

"Mum . . ."

"Yes?"

"Doesn't matter."

I peck her quickly on the cheek and go out the back way. As I shut the patio gate, I wave and then turn as if I am going in the direction of the Dog Leg.

Only the locals call it the Dog Leg. Its real name is the Cut, because that's what it is, a zigzag passage that acts as a shortcut between the Lane and Stanhope Avenue. Some people say it's called the Dog Leg because that's how it's shaped—like the back leg of a dog. Personally, I think that would make for one pretty deformed dog. The passage goes twenty yards east, then right-angles north for ten yards, then sharp east again for another ten and finally sharp north before coming out into daylight under the arch of two Stanhope Avenue houses, which are joined at the second-floor level like some architectural Siamese twins. Other people say the passage is called the Dog Leg because that's what happens there. Dogs lift their legs. At the lampposts. If only they knew.

There are two lampposts, not the concrete sort you see in ordinary streets, with the lozenge of orange light at the top, but ones that look as if they've come out of Narnia. Old-fashioned, fluted metal lampposts in pale green surmounted by hexagonal glass lamps which glimmer with that soft gas-mantle light. Sticking out horizontally, just below the lamp itself, is a fluted green metal arm with a bobble on the end, which looks like a place you might hang a coat if you were given to hanging your coat on a lamppost. Alternatively, if you were given to climbing lampposts this would be an excellent place to sit. It's where Niker sits. Niker climbs like a spider.

I didn't see him the first time, even though he was directly in front of me. I suppose that's because I was going along with my head at the five-foot level and he was perched another five feet above that. So when the first apple landed I thought it was just Norbert bad luck. Because, as it happens, there is this large Bramley apple tree on the first bend of the passage. In any case I wasn't exactly thinking of apple as ammunition, just apple as fruit, and fruit does occasionally fall off trees and hit people on account of the laws of gravity. So it was only when the second apple landed, squidgy and rotten and directly on my head, that I thought to look up. Or maybe it was the laugh that made me look. He's quite a good marksman, Niker, and I think he hit me another four times before I managed to turn the corner. Afterward, as I scraped the gunge off my coat with a stick, I wondered why I hadn't thought to return fire. But I think I would have missed anyway.

Of course the next time I went via the Dog Leg I checked the lamppost (which you can see from the entrance) before going in. Only that time he was up the second lamppost, the one you can't see until you turn the middle bend. This post doesn't have a convenient apple tree nearby. So he had a plastic bag. He was wearing gloves and he threw something loose and brown that splatted on the back of my neck. I thought it was mud—until I breathed in. When I got to school I washed it out of my hair, but the smell was still on my collar.

"Norbert," Niker said at Break. "Did anyone ever tell you, you stink?" He was sitting on the playground wall next to Kate, who was swinging her legs and eating string cheese. "You should take a bath." He jumped off the wall into a puddle, soaking me, but also himself.

"E-jit," Kate said, and laughed.

As soon as I got home that afternoon I changed and stuffed my shirt into the bottom of the laundry basket. But Mum has a nose like a bloodhound.

"What happened?" she asked.

"I fell over."

"On your back?"

"Yes."

"In a pile of dog muck?"

"Yes."

"Robert?"

"Yes, Mum, I fell over on my back. In a pile of dog muck. People do, you know."

As I bathed, I thought about what Kate meant by "E-jit." Or rather—who she meant. I decided she meant Niker and that's why I didn't stop using the Dog Leg. Not then anyway. No. I walked through it every day. Right up until the Grape Incident.

I'm not saying I wasn't scared. The Dog Leg's a spooky place anyway. Mum says it's not mortar that holds the walls together but graffiti. And the more often our neighbors creosote their back gates the more elaborate the spray painting gets. It makes the houses looked marked, as if all the victims from the Great Plague ended up with homes backing onto the Cut.

And then there's the broken glass and the smell of urine—and I don't mean dog urine either. Because dog urine doesn't smell, does it? And even though the passage is a perfectly ordinary path made of perfectly ordinary concrete, footfalls really echo there. There always seems to be someone behind you, or coming toward you. It's difficult to locate exactly where someone else is in the passage until you're right on them. Or they're on you. But then it should be safe because so many people use it: dog-walkers, shoppers, business-people on their way to the sandwich shop, everyday grown-ups going about their everyday business. So maybe it is only me that smells fear there.

The apple-throwing happened in the autumn. And it wasn't until the summer that Niker devised the grape thing. Eight months ago now, but it seems like yesterday. There were two new boys in class that term, Jon Pinkman and Shane Perkiss, Pinky and Perky, and he did it to them too. So it wasn't just me. I wasn't the only one. Pinky only stayed one term.

Anyway, I don't want to talk about that now. I just want to explain why it is that I head south today— toward the sea—instead of east toward school. It's one of about seven routes I use. I never decide in advance which way I'm going to go, on the basis that Niker still manages to intercept me on an unnerving number of occasions, so he either has to be psychic or he's put some sort of implant in my brain. If it's the implant then I reckon he can't know where I'm going until I know where I'm going, so the later I decide, the less time he has to get there before me. You could call it paranoid, but then anyone who's been through the Dog Leg with Pinky and Perky and a bunch of grapes has the right to be paranoid.

I make my route decision the moment I let the back-gate latch fall. Click—I'm going to the sea. Click—I'm going past the library. Only, to be honest, I do choose the sea more often than the other routes, because I love the sea. Especially in winter. Sometimes, when it's really rough, the sea throws pebbles onto the promenade, and walking there is like treading on fists.

Today I choose the sea, but I don't go as far as the prom, just down to the main road (where I stand a moment to look at the color of the waves) before turning inland again. It doesn't really matter which of the northerly roads I take, Occam, the Grove, St. Aubyns, they all arrive pretty much at the gasworks and then it's just a few hundred yards to school. Today I select St. Aubyns, which is a wide, ugly street with gargantuan four-floor buildings, most of which have now been turned into guest houses. One of them is called the Cinderella Hotel. It has a flight of ballroom-type steps up to its huge front door. And I'm looking, as I always do, for the glass slipper, when my eye is drawn to the building next door. It's a colossal edifice, grim, square, semiderelict. And, painted in gold on the glass above the boarded front door, are these words: Chance House, 26 St. Aubyns.

I read the words and then I read them again. After which I shut my eyes, turn a full circle, and open my eyes again. The words are still there. As they must have been every one of the hundred times I've walked up this street.

"You can go there. Walk. It's not far."

And of course I know it's Edith Sorrel's house because it is precisely what I have been expecting. It's the place I saw before I slept last night, the one I pretended to imagine. The one I knew was here but, perhaps, would rather not have known, which is why I suppose I chose to hear Edith Sorrel say "St. Albans" when her clear-as-a-bell voice actually said "St. Aubyns."

Do you sometimes feel drawn and repelled in the same moment? I call it the car-crash mentality—you don't want to look but you just can't help yourself. Even though you know you are going to see something appalling. Well, Chance House is my car crash. I've tried ignoring it but it won't go away. So now I'm going to have to look. Worse than that, I'm going to have to go in, though every sensible fiber in my body is willing me to walk away.

There are two bits of good news. One is that I have to be at school in less than ten minutes. The other is that Chance House is boarded up. And I don't just mean with a few nails and a bit of chipboard. Each of the eight-foot ground-floor windows has been secured with a sheet of steel-framed, steel-meshed fiberglass. The front door is barricaded with a criss-cross of steel bars, and although the second-floor windows are not obstructed, they are twenty feet from any handhold I can see. Of course it could be different around the back.

I look up the road and then down the road. No one is watching. No one I can see anyway. I slip into the shadow of the side of the house. Grass sprouts through the concrete paving. There's a small door, set into the wall of the house about four feet above ground level. It's not barred but it doesn't look like it has to be. There are no steps to it, and as well as being overgrown with brambles, it's swollen shut, rotted into its doorframe.

I advance, slowly, toward the back of the house, as if I'm scared of the corner. As if I expect someone to be lying in wait, just out of view. My heart pounds as I walk. But I can't stop now. I come to the edge of the house, just one more step, I turn . . .

The garden is empty, overgrown. There are dandelions in the long grass. Bluebells and a smashed white-wine bottle. The sun is remarkably warm. I compose my breathing. There is steel mesh on the first window. And on the second. There is no way I will be able to get into the house.

And then I see it. French doors onto the garden. The mesh hanging free, ripped from the wall as if it were paper.

I don't know who's moving my legs but I'm going toward that open door. Walking fast now, past the dirty Sainsbury's bag and the length of washing line, past the patch of scorched earth where someone has lit a fire. Of course, if the door is open there will be people. Squatters, vagrants, drug addicts. Who knows? My heart's back at it again. Bang, bang, bang. Like my rib cage is a drum. What am I going to tell these people? That I've come because some batty old lady asked me to? I should be creeping, slithering along the walls like they do in the movies. But I'm not. I'm walking with the boldness of the bit-part guy who gets shot. Somebody screams, and for a moment I think it's me. But actually it's a seagull, wheeling overhead.

My legs are still on remote control but there's something wrong with my breathing. I seem to have lost the knack of it. I instruct myself to breathe normally. In out, in out. The "out" seems OK, but the "in" is too quick and too shallow. How long does it take a person to die of oxygen starvation anyway? In out, in out. I've come to the door. In.

In. The room has been stripped. There are brackets but no cupboards, the dust shape of what might have been a boiler, plumbing for a sink that isn't there and a mad array of cut and dangling wires. On the left-hand wall is a rubble hole where a fireplace has been gouged out and the floor is strewn with paper, envelopes and smashed brick.

At the far end of the room is a glass door. An internal door which must lead to the rest of the house. I look behind me and then I step inside. The door's closed but obviously not locked because someone has put a brick at its foot, to stop it swinging. A final look over my shoulder and I'm moving toward that door. But I've only gone a couple of paces when I hear the scraping. A rhythmic, deliberate noise that stops me dead. The sort of noise you'd make if you were watching someone and wanted them to know you were watching, without yourself being seen.

Scrape, scrape, scrape. Pause. Scrape.

It's coming from my right. From the small kitchen window over the absent sink. This window is almost opaque, darkened by the steel-mesh glass and the shadow of some bush or tree that's growing too close to the house.

Scrape. Pause. Scrape.

I see the finger now. And the knuckle—which looks deformed. But perhaps that's just the trick of the light, the refraction of bone through fiberglass. My heart is beating like a warrior drum. Tom tom tom tom tom tom. But I'm not going to panic. I'm emphatically not going to panic.

I panic.

I leap out of the room into the garden.

I scream: "I can see you!"

A holly bush continues to scrape one of its branches against the glass of the kitchen window. Scrape. Pause. Scrape. In time with the wind.

I'm so relieved I sob. Huge foolish tears rolling down my cheeks. Norbert No-Brain. Norbert No-Bottle. At least Niker isn't here to see. Or Kate. When the boo-hooing stops I look for a hanky. But I don't have one so I pick a dock leaf and blow my nose on that.

Right. That's it. I'm going back in. I make for the glass door. I stride there, kick the brick out of the way and go through into a narrow corridor. Then I worry about the brick. If anyone sees the brick's been moved, they'll know someone's in the house. I go back out into the kitchen (which, compared with the corridor, is light and airy and pleasant) and retrieve the brick. Then I discover I can't shut the door with me on the inside and the brick on the outside. Or I can, just, if I squeeze my fingers around the gap between door and doorpost, edging the brick back into place. Hang on, what if someone jams the brick right up against the door, barricading me in? Change of plan. Better to have the brick on my side of the door after all. That way at least if someone comes in from the garden, they'll knock it over getting into the house and I'll hear them. I bring the brick in, lean it against the door my side. Now I'm safe. If the people are outside.

But what if they're inside?

I look at my watch. Six minutes to nine. I really have to get to school. Absolutely can't be late. Have to go right now. The skirting board in the corridor has been ripped off. There's a gap between the base of the wall and the floorboards through which I can see down to some sort of basement. In the dark cavity there are flowerpots, lamp bases, lampshades, a desk, a filing cabinet and a sink, the old ceramic sort. There's also the sound of water. Not a small drip drip, but a gushing, the noise of a tap on full bringing water pouring from a tank. Or maybe a cistern filling, or a bath emptying or . . .

Crash!

It's the brick. The brick has fallen. I wheel around, catch my foot in the hole in the floor, fall, twist my ankle, drag myself up, never once taking my eyes from the swinging door. But nobody comes through. Nobody comes through! Why don't they come through! I'm not an impetuous person, but I burst through that door, hopping across the kitchen faster than normal people run. And then I'm in the garden, and actually my ankle's all right, so I do run. Run, run, run—flowers, washing line, burnt ground, smashed glass, corner of house, swollen door, front wall. Front wall of Chance House. Safety of St. Aubyns. I collapse onto the pavement.

" 'Run rabbit, run rabbit, run run run.' " A familiar voice croons softly above me. " 'Don't be afraid of the farmer's gun.' "

I look up. About a hand's breadth from my head is a pair of feet.

"Hello, Norbert," says Niker.

He swings himself down from the wall.

"You want to watch yourself." He brushes imaginary specks of dust from his trousers. "Bad place, Chance House." He smiles.

"What?"

"Bad place, Norbert. Bad house. Bad karma."

He looks at my blank face. "You don't know, do you? Everyone in town knows. But you don't." He turns toward school.

"Niker . . ."

He pauses. "Yes, Norbert?"

"Tell me."

"Please. Pretty please, Norbert."

"Pretty please."

He looks at me pityingly. "A boy died in there, Norbert."

"What?"

"You heard."

"What boy? Who?"

"Just a boy, Norbie. Pasty little thing, by all accounts. Fluffy hair. Pale. Pocked. Bit like you, really. But his mum couldn't see it. Doted on him, apparently. Told him he was wonderful. So wonderful he could fly. So what does he do? Opens the window of the top-floor flat and gives it a go. Pretty nasty mess on the concrete by all accounts."

"Top floor? Top-Floor Flat, Chance House? Are you sure?"

"You feeling all right, Norbert?"

"Niker, are you sure?"

"Higher the window, more the strawberry jam. Lots of strawberry jam in this boy's case, Norbert. Top-Floor Flat for certain." He grins. "Come on now, bunny, you're going to be late for school. Better hop it, eh?"

I remain sitting on the pavement.

"Suit yourself." He turns away.

As I watch his retreating back, the little swagger in his step, I want to believe it's all just a story. One he's made up to frighten me. But I know that what's really frightened me is Chance House itself. You see, it smells like the Dog Leg. It smells of fear.

5

Let me tell you about Kate. She's slim and has a small round face with a pointed chin and freckles over the bridge of her nose. Her hair is light brown and straight and she keeps it cut short, usually with bangs. Her eyes are hazel, and when she smiles, a little dimple appears in her right cheek. Niker says she looks like a cat. She's my idea of an angel.

It took me two terms to pluck up courage to invite her to my house. I chose a Friday, because that's a day I know she's normally free. Both times she went back with Niker it was a Friday.

"Thanks for asking, Robert," she said. "But I can't. I'm busy." She smiled and I watched the dimple appear.

"Fine," I said. "Another time maybe."

"Sure."

But I didn't ask again. When someone says they're busy, you never know if they're really busy or just busy for you. And I thought if I asked again I might find out. And perhaps I didn't want to find out. Besides, it was clear I had left the door open. She could invite herself anytime. But she didn't.

So you can imagine how I feel when, next time we get onto the minibus to visit the Mayfield Rest Home, Kate chooses to sit by me. OK, so it's not exactly a free choice. She's late and there are only two seats left, one next to student teacher and damp sponge Liz Finch, the other next to me. On the other hand, I have the seat over the wheel with the restricted legroom and Miss Finch has the front seat with the view. So if Kate's just looking for somewhere to sit, Finch's seat is closer and comfier. So I reckon it has to be significant that it is at my feet that Kate dumps her bag.

"Hi," I say.

"Hello," she replies.

I once set the dream alarm on Kate. Lay on my back in bed and asked myself how to make that

dimple come more often for me. At 3 A.M. I was
dreaming that a boy was throwing stones in a lake.
Every time he hit the surface it made a dimple. The
water was radiating dimples. But the boy wasn't me. I
left it alone after that.

Hey—but who cares about the past? Right now
Kate Barber is sitting next to me. The journey to the
Mayfield Rest Home is ten minutes. I spend two of
those ten minutes trying to open my mouth, which
seems to have got stuck on closed. I want to say stuff
like: Did anyone ever tell you how insanely beautiful
you are, Kate? But even I can see that's nerdy, and I
don't want her opinion of me to drop from wood
louse to unicellular organism. So, after four minutes
(Kate's reading her book now), I say:

"Do you know anything about Chance House?"

"Sorry?"

"Chance House, twenty-six St. Aubyns." It's not
such a wild remark. Kate lives on Oakwood, which is
just two roads from St. Aubyns. "That big house that's
all boarded up?"

"No." Kate returns to her book.

"Spooky. Spooky, spooky, creepy, spooky." Wesley
Parr's face appears around my headrest. "Boy died in
dat dere housie, Norbert No-Chance." He looks at
Kate. "Norbert No-Chance-at-All."

"Oh, that house," says Kate.

"Boy about your littlie, littlie age, Norbert," says Weasel.

"So about your age too then, Weasel," says Kate smartly.

"Oh, creepy, creepy, bye-bye, spooky." Weasel's head disappears.

"So you do know?"

"Not really," says Kate. "Or only as much as everyone knows. That a boy is supposed to have died there. And that it's never been much of a lucky house since. Keeps changing hands."

"Who was the boy?"

"I don't know. It was ages ago, Robert."

"How many ages?"

"Thirty years. Forty years. I don't know. Why are you so interested anyway?"

"My Elder, Edith Sorrel. She lived there."

"Oh, right. Why don't you ask her then?"

"Mm. Maybe I will."

But of course I won't. Can you imagine it?

Me: "Oh, hello, Miss Sorrel, would you mind telling me about the boy who died in your house? I mean the one that fell out of the top-floor window? The plenty strawberry jam one?"

Her (giving me that witchy look where she appears to be able to see right through me and out the other side): "No."

End of conversation. But not end of story. Miss Sorrel picks up silver-topped ebony cane, bangs it three times on floor and kazzam! I'm a frog. That would be the happy ending. The miserable one would be the ending where—

"Robert. Robert!"

The bus has stopped. Almost everyone has got off.

"Robert Nobel, you are a dreamer." Miss Finch is waving her hands in front of my face. She looks almost animated.

I pick up my bags and follow the others into the lounge of the Mayfield Rest Home. Today Catherine has arrived in advance of us. She has set up trestle tables with paper, paint, pencils, scissors, magazines and glue. The protective newspaper she's laid on the carpet is already rucked up with the traffic of wheelchairs.

"Hello, hello," she says. "Come in. Find your Elder, everyone. Sit down."

There is a hubbub of greetings.

"Afternoon, Mr. Root," says Kate.

"Eh up," says Albert.

"How you been, Dulcie?" says Weasel.

"What?" says Dulcie.

"Hi," says Niker, tapping Mavis on the chicken-wing shoulder.

"Please explain," says Mavis. "Don't keep me guessing."

"It's me," says Niker. "Me, *moi,* myself. Niker. Jonathan Niker. Double O one and a half."

"Oh," says Mavis. "Is that a poultice?"

"Could be," says Niker.

"Sit down, sit down," calls Catherine gaily. "Sit down by your Elder, please, everyone."

But I have no Elder. Edith Sorrel is not in the room. I remain standing.

"Sit down, Robert. It is Robert, isn't it?"

I sit.

Behind me Niker sets up a soft hum. *Do, do der doo, do der do der do der doo.* It's a funeral march. "Never mind, Norbie," he whispers. "I'm sure it wasn't your fault." *Do, do der doo . . .*

"Quiet now, please. Well, today I hope we're going to move on to actually making some work," says Catherine. "Some little illustrations of the wisdoms that we were talking about last week. I was speaking to Albert before you all arrived and he mentioned paths to me . . ."

"Primrose path to hell," squawks Mavis.

"Right on," says Niker.

"Well," says Catherine, "I think Albert was thinking more of paths of wisdom. And path as visual image. Which I thought was a very good idea. Because paths are things that lead us on, take us from one place to another. So perhaps that could be our starting point for today. We might think of an individual paving stone, perhaps with a wisdom inscribed on it, or something growing round it, or something or someone treading on the stone. . . . You can use any of the materials here and . . ."

People begin to drift toward the tables. In the noise and movement I slip away into the corridor. I remember exactly where Edith Sorrel's room is. Third on the right. I knock softly, in case she's asleep. There is no answer. Quietly, I ease open the door. The room is small and institutional. There are a bed, a chair, a wardrobe, a basin and a bedside cabinet. Except for a toothbrush, facecloth and soap, there are no personal items at all: no photos, no china, no knickknacks, not even a book.

Miss Sorrel is asleep, breathing quietly and evenly. Sitting in the chair at the bottom of her bed is a man.

He rises, as if startled by me. He's tall and white-haired and, despite the heat of the room, he's wearing a full-length black overcoat. There's something hunched about him, something glittering, that makes me think crow, hooded crow. He stares like I owe him an explanation, so I say:

"Hello, I'm Robert. I'm on the project."

"Ernest," he replies edgily. "Ernest Sorrel."

"Oh," I say. "You must be her brother then."

"No. Not exactly." His eyes bore into me. "I'm her husband."

I try to keep my face neutral but, as Edith Sorrel told me quite emphatically that she didn't have a husband, it isn't easy.

"No doubt she didn't mention me?" He smiles, or maybe it's a grimace, and then he sits again, his coat curling around his legs.

"I'm sure she would have done," I say uncomfortably. "I mean if we'd talked about things like that. But we didn't. We just sort of talked about the project."

"Oh. And what project's that, Robert?"

"The art project. About your lives and ours."

"Mm?"

"The similarities or differences."

No reply.

"Stories." I'm burbling. Why don't I just quit? Leave? He's obviously not interested. So why are my feet stuck to the floor? "Wisdoms. You know."

"I see."

"She said about Chance House."

"What!" His detached tone vanishes instantly. He appears astounded. "She spoke of Chance House?"

I nod.

"Oh." He turns toward her. "Oh, Edith." He stretches out, as if to touch her, but his reaching hand falls short.

"What did she say?" he asks me.

"Just sort of mentioned it."

"Mentioned what exactly?"

"Chance House."

"No." He gives a violent shake of the head. "Edith could not have 'just mentioned' Chance House. It's over thirty years since she was last able to say the words 'Chance House.'"

I shrug. He doesn't look like the sort of person you contradict.

"Thirty-four years and three months, to be precise."

"I ought to go."

"No. No . . ." And then he adds, "Please."

His desperation is sudden and disconcerting.

"I need to know. What did she say? Exactly. You have to tell me."

That's when he goes flimsy. Or that's how it seems to me. As if his huge coat is just a piece of black cloth wrapped around nothing. As if, were I to blow at this moment, he would simply collapse inward, disappear. Which is why I try to remember for him, to be as exact as I can.

"Well, I asked her what the most important thing in her life was. I had to ask, it was part of the project that—"

"Yes, yes, and . . ."

"And she said, without any hesitation: 'Chance House.'"

"That's all?"

"No. 'Top-Floor Flat. Chance House. Twenty-six St. Aubyns.'"

"Did she seem . . ." He pauses. ". . . agitated at all? Upset?"

"No. She just said it normally. Like it was just the place you lived."

"No. We never lived there."

"What?"

"We never lived in Chance House." He laughs a low, miserable laugh. "Never *lived* there."

"I ought to go. They'll be wondering where I am."

Ernest Sorrel stands up. "Is there anything else? I have to know."

"No."

Again that look—both demanding and needy.

"OK then. Yes. She asked me to go there."

"To go to Chance House?"

"Yes."

"How old are you, Robert?"

"Twelve. Nearly thirteen."

"His age," Ernest Sorrel whispers. "And his height."

"Whose age? Whose height?"

"Robert"—he puts his hand on my arm—"please don't go to the house."

"But she asked me to," I say, suddenly stubborn. "And I said I would."

"Edith is ill. Has been ill a long time. But now it's different. It's serious, Robert. She could . . . she could . . . I don't want her hurt any more. I don't want her to hurt. You understand me?"

His hand is still on my arm. It looks like a claw. "She said she didn't have a husband," I say.

He releases me. "Yes. And she probably said she didn't have a son either."

He sees by my face that he has caught me out. "We all remember things, Robert. And forget them. Memory is, you see, a very selective thing."

In the bed Edith stirs. Now it is Ernest's turn to be caught out. He gathers himself quickly. "Goodbye, Robert."

"You're going?"

He's almost out the door.

"Do you want me to tell her you were here?"

I think he shakes his head, but I can't be sure because of how quickly he closes the door.

Edith wakes.

"Robert," she says. Lying down she doesn't seem so witchy. Her white hair is mussed and the lines on her face gentle. She smiles at me. "It's my Robert, isn't it?"

Does she really look different, or is it just what Ernest has said about her being ill that makes me look at her differently?

"Hello, Miss Sorrel."

She pulls herself upright. She's wearing a pale pink negligee with a ruffle of pink ribbon about the neck.

"I'm sorry to barge in," I continue. "Only it's the project and we're supposed to be making some work today and–"

"Have you been to the house?" She interrupts, nice Gran suddenly going hard round the edges.

I pause. "Sort of."

"And?" She leans forward.

"It's all boarded up."

Her still-dark eyebrows knit across her brow. "So?"

"You can't get in."

She gives me that see-right-through-you look. "You can do anything," she says, "if you want to enough."

I'm not fast enough to say, "But do I want to, do I really want to go into that house?" So she says:

"Pass me my stick!"

I hand her the ebony cane with the silver top. She throws back her covers, swings her feet to the edge of the bed and bangs the stick on the floor. I check my face and hands. No scaly throat. No webbed fingers.

"Dressing-gown!"

I find the pink quilted affair in the cupboard. She refuses my help to put it on. Pulls it around her angry body. Jerks and twists at the belt, while I watch uselessly. "There!" Finally she has some sort of knot. She smiles triumphantly.

"I could have been a singer," she announces, as

though we're in the middle of an argument about the subject. "I had a beautiful voice. Everyone said so. 'You must train that voice,' they said. But he wouldn't let me. Said it wasn't a suitable occupation for a woman. I wasn't to do it. Even though I had a place at college. I had to give it up. Wasn't to sing." She turns to me, eyes ablaze. "But I did."

"Right," I say. And then, "Who wouldn't let you?"

"Pardon?"

"Who didn't want you to sing?"

"Ernest, of course. My husband."

Well, that figures. "I thought you said you didn't have a husband."

"I don't. Not anymore."

"Oh—you divorced." Then Ernest's claw dissolves into Ernest's tender, reaching hand and I suddenly feel the way I do when my dad rings me from some far-away place and tries to make conversation, and it all sounds false and forced and I want to be able to do something about it but I can't.

"Yes. We parted. He went away."

"But you still see each other," I say tentatively.

"Of course not."

"He doesn't visit?"

"Why should he? I haven't seen him for thirty years."

And then I think she must be ill and that's what

makes her forget. Because she can't not know that he sits at the end of her bed watching and–

"So you'll go then?" she says.

"I'm sorry?"

"You'll go to Chance House, go to the top, Top-Floor Flat?"

"Miss Sorrel, what is it you want from the house?"

"Want? I want you to go in."

"But why?"

She looks suddenly bewildered. "Because . . ."

"It's boarded up. I told you. It's derelict."

"But you can go in," she says with slight desperation.

"Yes. OK. You're right. There is a way in."

"Yes?"

"And I did go in. But I was afraid. I was terrified. In fact I didn't even get past the kitchen."

"Robert." She stretches out a bony hand, clasps it over mine. "You must not be afraid. Do you understand me? You are a wonderful boy. An extraordinary boy. You can do anything you want. You can fly, Robert."

I snatch my hand away. "What?"

"I said, you are the sort of boy who can fly." She smiles. "So you will go for me, won't you?"

"No. No!"

"But you must. I beg you."

"What's in there, Miss Sorrel? What do you expect me to find?"

"Find?" The confusion is back. She concentrates, draws in her lips. "I don't know."

"You must know, if it's so important to you."

"I don't know." She says this coldly, shutting me out. "I don't remember."

Out in the hall a clock strikes. In the silence that follows I hear Catherine's voice from the lounge beyond.

"Shall we finish with a song, then?"

There's some mumbling and scuffling and clearing of throats. Then it begins, a few cracked old voices, led by warbling Albert, and the stronger but not necessarily more tuneful tones of my classmates:

"'One man went to mow, went to mow a meadow . . .'"

"Who's doing that?" demands Edith.

"'Went to mow a meadow, two men, one man and his dog, went to mow a meadow . . .'"

The song is lifting now, louder as more voices join in.

"I told them to stop. Make them stop." Edith is banging her cane. Banging and banging. "Tell them to stop, Robert!"

"Does it hurt your ears?"

"No! It hurt, it hurts . . . I don't know! I don't remember!"

She drops her cane and puts her arms over her head. I'd like to think she's hiding. But actually I think she's sobbing. Big silent sobs. And I don't know how to comfort her so I just stand there. And then the crying gets worse, or maybe it doesn't get worse, it just goes on. It doesn't stop. So finally I say: "OK. OK. I'll go. If it means that much to you, I'll go."

She lifts her head. "You are such a dear boy," she says.

6

It's warm during the days but cold at night. I'm sitting in front of an empty grate. Dad used to light the fires. In fact it was something we used to do together. He showed me how to roll the newspaper and tie it into a loose knot, how to lay the kindling and space the smaller pieces of coal. After he left, Mum said lighting the fire was too much trouble. It meant too much clearing up. She didn't have the time. So I laid a fire once. I did it just as he taught me. I thought Mum would be pleased. But when she got home she went mad. What did I think I was doing with the matches!

I could have burnt the house down! But she was wrong. The fire wouldn't light. It sputtered and went out. Just charred sticks in the grate.

I want to light a fire now. Or maybe I just want to have a fire lit. Which is different of course, and involves my dad walking through the door and doing it. Which he won't. Not least because he lives sixty miles away and can't visit often. He has a new family now. Jo's two girls (Annabelle, who's older than me, and Louise, who's just younger) and the new baby, Lewis. Lewis must be about one and a half now. My stepbrother. I've only seen him once. I sent him a tower of stacking cups for his first birthday. I bought them with my own money. It's on account of having so many new birth dates to remember that Dad sometimes forgets mine, Mum says. The last present Dad actually gave me on the day was the soldiers for my eighth birthday. I wouldn't swap them for anything in the world now. But then I was disappointed. I'd wanted an airplane. One I could make fly. Ride the wind. You see, I've always dreamed of being a pilot. I let that slip to Niker once.

"They don't train blind people for pilots," he said, wibbling my glasses up and down on my nose.

I asked Mum if that was true.

"I think there are certainly strict medicals," she said.

I took that to mean they don't train blind people like me. And I haven't mentioned it since. But I still have my dreams and in my dreams I fly. Not in a plane but with my arms outstretched, gliding, swooping, rising and falling with the hot air currents. And it feels good. It feels powerful. I never feel that power when I'm awake. Awake I am something feeble. Something laughed at.

Of course I'm thinking about Edith Sorrel's words: "You can fly, Robert. You are the sort of boy who can fly."

And of course I'm also thinking of Niker's story of the boy who tried to fly from 26 St. Aubyns and fell to his strawberry-jam death. And while I know it's only a coincidence—because Edith didn't mean what she said literally, did not expect me to take off and fly about her room, and Niker's story was just that, a story—I cannot help feeling the connection. And that's another reason why I'm going to go to the top of Chance House. Because it feels personal. Not just Edith Sorrel's story but mine too.

"Penny for them."

"Hello, Mum."

She ruffles my hair. "You didn't hear me come in, did you?"

"No."

"You must have a very vivid inner life." She sits down. "Go on then, what were you thinking about?"

"Nothing."

She raises an eyebrow.

"Selective memory."

"What?"

"Selective memory, what is it?"

"Selective memory is when I tell you you can have a chocolate biscuit if you tidy your room, and you remember to take the biscuit but forget to tidy your room."

"Seriously, Mum."

"I am being serious. That's what it is. Choosing to remember some things and forget others. And it normally involves remembering the good things and forgetting the bad. Why do you want to know?"

"Someone accused my Elder of having a selective memory."

"Who?"

"Her husband."

"Oh well—there are lots of things between husbands and wives you'd want to forget."

"Like that time on the landing, when Dad smashed the dish?" I don't know why I say this. I don't know why it's on my mind.

She looks at me. "No. I'm not likely to forget that." There's a pause. "I'm sorry. I didn't even know you knew."

I shrug.

"I thought you were asleep." She sighs. "Guess it

was difficult to be asleep. Right? Maybe I just wanted you to be asleep. Maybe that's the selective memory bit." She smiles. "OK?"

"OK."

"It's normally the really bad stuff that your brain edits out," she continues. "Shows that the thing between Dad and me can't really have been that bad. Just a dish, see?"

She waits for me to nod.

"Take the war. Men 'forget' the terrible killing they saw. Your great-granddad—my granda—it was like that for him. Never wanted to talk about the trenches. He was at the Somme, you know. He lived and others died. It's difficult, being a survivor. You feel guilty."

She pulls her cardigan tighter about her. "Getting chilly, isn't it? Maybe it's the gloomy talk. What would you say to a hot chocolate?"

"Good evening, hot chocolate." That was one of Dad's jokes. Both of us laugh limply and she goes into the kitchen.

I don't want to compare the Grape Incident to the Great War, but this is what I'm thinking. Maybe I have selective memory about this. Maybe refusing to talk about what happened is my way of refusing to think about it. But the Grape Incident keeps popping into my brain, keeps on nagging. Like Chance House nagged. Then I wonder two things: first—did the

Somme nag Great-grandpa Cutting? Second—what exactly is it that's nagging Edith Sorrel?

I follow Mum into the kitchen and watch the gas hiss under the pan of milk.

"How does old age affect memory?" I ask.

"Generally speaking, you just become increasingly forgetful. Just last week I managed to leave my purse in the house. . . ."

"No. Really old people."

"Short-term memory," says Mum. "That's what normally goes first. A person won't be able to tell you what they had for breakfast, whereas they will be able to describe in perfect detail an event that happened fifty years ago."

"Does that mean," I venture, "that if you'd tried to forget something, something that happened to you, say, thirty years ago, you might suddenly 're-member' it in old age?"

"You mean a bad memory?" Mum asks. "Something you'd actively tried to suppress?"

"Yes."

"I'm not sure. I think you can bury stuff so deep you never uncover it."

"So if you did begin to remember," I press, "then some part of you must want to find out, want to examine the horrid thing?"

"What are you getting at, Robert?"

"Nothing. Just asking."

"Has old Mrs. Sorrel got some skeleton in the cupboard?"

"Old Miss Sorrel," I say.

"I thought you said she had a husband?"

"She has someone who says he is her husband."

"Oh—and what does she say?"

I'm still considering this when, in the front room, the phone rings.

The milk is on the boil. "Can you get that for me, Robert?"

I go to the phone.

"Hello?"

"Hello, Robert."

"Hello, Dad," I whisper. If Mum knows it's him she'll come, milk or no milk.

"All right?"

"Fine."

"Good day at school?"

"Great."

Silence.

"Ahem." Dad coughing.

"All right, Dad?"

"Course. Fine."

Sometimes I blame him. That he never asks the right questions. That we only ever talk at this useless monosyllabic level. Then I think it must be me. That I don't give the right answers. That I should say: Actually I'm not all right because it's cold and you're not here to lay a fire. And school wasn't great either because I met Ernest Sorrel at the home, and I don't want to believe that the boy who fell out of the Top-Floor Flat of Chance House was Edith Sorrel's son, because she said she didn't have a son. But then she said she didn't have a husband either. And I feel quite frightened because I'm going to go to the top of a derelict house and I want someone to tell me not to go, but no one knows I'm going so they can't. And by the way, does my mind run round in circles like this because I'm mad? Or because Niker really has got an implant in my brain? And Dad, Dad, were you ever frightened of a boy at school? I mean really frightened? And—

"Robert?"

"Yes?"

"Can you get your mother?"

"Mum—it's Dad." I put down the receiver. Then I pick it up again. "Are we going to see you Saturday?"

"That's what I want to speak to your mother about."

Mum comes into the room with two steaming mugs of chocolate. They smell of the time when Dad and Mum and I used to sit together in front of a blazing winter fire.

"Hello, Nigel. Yes. No. I see."

Mum's mouth goes into a tight line. He's telling her something she doesn't want to hear. And I know what it is. There's some problem about Saturday. One of the children–Dad's new children–is ill maybe. Or there's a clash with an appointment of Jo's, she needs the car. It's all off. He isn't coming.

"Right," says Mum. "Well, I think it's important for Robert that we make another time, don't you? Have you got your diary?"

"Don't bother," I say. "Don't bother. It doesn't matter."

"Robert . . . ," she calls after me.

But I'm away. I'm up the stairs and in my bedroom with the door shut and wedged.

Mum will follow me. She always does. Tries to comfort me. But what good is that? The way I look at it is–I'm on my own. So I'd better get used to it.

7

I arrive at Chance House at 8:25 A.M. I considered coming after school, to give myself more time. But then I thought—what if something goes wrong? With Mum at work, it could be hours before anyone even notices I'm missing, let alone institutes a search. Whereas I reckon if I'm more than fifteen minutes late for morning school, Miss Raynham will have the tracker dogs out.

I don't go round the back of the house. Not immediately anyway. I stride boldly up the front steps, advertising my presence in the hope that Niker will jump out of some bush. But he doesn't. Never there when you want him, Niker. There's a man emptying rubbish outside the Cinderella Hotel next door and I look to him too, needing him to challenge me, call me a trespasser, rail about the despicable youth of today and threaten me with the police if I don't vamoose PDQ. But, no. He just shuts the lid of his dustbin and goes back inside.

So I'm forced to come down the steps and start walking. I go round the side, past the door rotted into its frame and overgrown with brambles, past the beer can . . . Beer can? I don't remember any beer can. Up to the corner of the house now and then on, round– into the abandoned garden. The dandelions are still there, and the bluebells, the smashed wine bottle, the dirty Sainsbury's bag (now wind-hooked on the branch of a tree), the washing line, the scorched earth and the microwave. Microwave. The microwave is definitely new. I couldn't have missed a microwave. Could I? I half hope the mesh will have been screwed back over the kitchen door and that all access will be denied. But of course the mesh is off and the kitchen wide open.

I look up. The top-floor windows give nothing away. They are blank. But no more blank than those of the Cinderella Hotel next door. What exactly am I expecting? It not as though there's going to be a body up there. If there were to be a body it should be down here. I look at the concrete beneath my feet. Plain ordinary concrete with a few blades of grass pushing through the cracks. Pushing up the daisies. Maybe he's under there after all, the boy, pushing up the daisies, forcing those cracks, erupting from the soil beneath. . . .

Robert Nobel. You are an idiot. You are Norbert No-Brain. It is just a story. Niker's story. And anyway the boy would just be worms now. It all happened—if it happened—so long ago.

Last night I couldn't sleep. Was thinking about the flat, Edith Sorrel, the boy, the strawberry jam over and over—and then I dreamed . . . No. Forget that. It was only a dream. A story—just a story like the other story. Concentrate on getting into the house. Please, just get into the house!

I get in.

It's not windy today and the holly bush is not scraping the window. I step over the litter of paper, the envelopes, the fireplace rubble. The inner kitchen door is closed, the brick up against it. Nothing seems touched. But I touched that brick, I moved it into the corridor, then pelted back through the kitchen door, leaving the brick where it had fallen, on the other side. So someone has been in. Someone has put the brick back in its place.

Quietly, I move the brick and enter the inner house. Through the gap between the floorboards and the wall I see again the basement mounds of lamps and flowerpots, the filing cabinet, the ceramic sink. They too look undisturbed. Yet something is different. I stand still. The water. There is no sound of gushing water. No sound of water at all in fact, not even a drip. I don't want to think about an explanation for this, because it has to involve people, other people, and—

Creak. Cre-eeak.

It could be the sound of me, because I've started walking again and the bare floorboards are bowed here, so they could be creaking. But they're not. The creak is in some other part of the house. Or maybe outside. It could well be outside. It's the sound they put in the movies when someone's hanging on the gallows and they don't want to show the body so they just have this creak. Creak. No—that's just my imagination. It doesn't sound like that at all. It sounds like feet. Someone moving in the house above me. And . . . and . . . I've arrived at the hall. A big, spacious entrance hall with a patterned tile floor: red, brown, yellow, terra-cotta, powder blue. At intervals groups of tiles are broken—not cracked but shattered, as though they've been smashed with a sledgehammer.

Creak.

Four doors lead off this hall. Three of them are

shut. I have to get to the stairs, so I can put my back against the wall. I'm far too exposed standing here. Anyone could come from any direction. So why aren't I moving anymore, why am I standing here completely still, paralyzed? Because I'm afraid, because if I step in the wrong place, I'll send tile shards skidding, then they'll know from the noise that I'm here, and they'll come for me–

Creak.

It's definitely upstairs. Up the stairs where I'm going. And I am going now. My feet are moving, skirting the smashed tiles, swiftly, almost silently.

Creak.

That was me. First foot on the stair and it creaks. So the other creaking must be the stairs too. Must be a person. I put my back against the wall. It's hard, bumpy, gritty. All the wallpaper has been ripped off and strewn on the stairs. So much paper it's difficult to see where the stair treads are. So there can't be people. If there were people going up and down, then the paper would be trodden flat, wouldn't it?

Dream. This is what I dreamed. Wallpaper. White going red. I dreamed that something murderous had happened in the house next door to ours in Grantley Street, and though it had happened many years ago, the house remembered and bled. And, because the house is one in a row, the bleeding came through the wall. The wallpaper in my room was soaked red. A spreading crimson stain which got bigger and bigger until—

Creak.

Half-landing. Something horrible and white and spongy and I'm treading on it. Wallpaper? No. Can't be. Wallpaper is not this thick. I lift my foot and put it down again—my shoe sinks in. Deep. What is it? Some plastic-coated giant bandage? No, no—stop panicking—it's just lagging. Just an abandoned old piece of lagging that used to go round a hot-water tank. Don't ask why it's here. You don't need to know. Turn off your thinking button. Just keep going. Keep your back against the wall. And breathe. Remember to breathe.

Creak.

Second floor. Creaks must be outside. Otherwise they'd be getting louder, wouldn't they? Or different anyway. Besides, if they were really footsteps, someone would appear. You can't walk round a house indefinitely. Walk, walk, walk, I mean, where would you be going?

Creak.

Fire door. Hardened glass door in the middle of the stairs blocking my way to the Top-Floor Flat, Chance House. No-Chance House. No chance of getting through the large, shut fire door. Thank God. It's shutting me out. Shutting Edith's secret in. I give the door a gentle push. There's the suck of an air vacuum and it opens.

A flight of stairs. Twelve small steps, that's all. And me, with my very small brain, going up them. Thump. Thump. Thump. That's not my feet on the bare treads, that's my heart banging in my chest. Bang, bang, bang, all the way up to the top. And at the top another door. The door of the flat itself.

It's open.

"Hello," I whisper.

Who am I expecting to answer? The ghost of the boy? A man with a beer can? A guy who has a thing about bricks.

"I can see you." Even quieter.

No one answers.

I go in.

The layout of the hallway is similar to that of the ground floor, only smaller—a central square with doors leading off. Four of the doors are wide open and one half open. Without moving, this is what I can see: to my left the ripped-out remains of a kitchen; directly in front of me a bathroom, the white toilet and basin both sledgehammered; to the left of that a totally bare room which might have been a living room; and to the right, a room stripped of everything but flowery wallpaper and a mattress. A bedroom presumably.

The room with the half-open door is the one that

looks over the back of the house, the one I know I have to go into, because it's from that room that you would have to jump if you were going to land on the concrete. Because of the angle of the door, I can see very little from where I'm standing. But I can see the wallpaper. It's children's paper. Babies' paper even. A jaunty, if faded, mother duck with three little ducklings in tow. The pattern repeated over and over. That room must contain a million mother ducks and her little ducklings.

What else does it contain?

I have goose bumps. The hairs on my forearms are standing upright, and those on the back of my neck feel like spikes. It's not cold but there's something icy rippling up and down my spine. I think it's fear. Although it could be terror. There's also something drumming in my ears. If I had to guess, I'd say it was the muffled panic of my own blood, because my hand is on the door handle of the room and I'm opening it, I'm pushing the whole weight of my body into the room where a boy just my age is supposed to have thrown himself to his death.

And now I'm in. I'm standing in the room, shaking from head to foot, my teeth knocking together like skittles in a bowling alley. And what's in the room?

Nothing. Absolutely nothing. No furniture, no light fittings, no carpet, no bodies. Not a single body.

Nothing but the million ducks, the three million duck-lings and a window. Yes. A window. A window over-looking the garden. Overlooking the concrete. The window has two large panes. One is smashed. A sharp cutout star of broken glass.

And of course I'm going toward it to check if it's large enough for a boy to have fallen through. Even though I know the idea is absurd, because why not open the window? Eh? Why not, if you want to get out? Why chuck yourself through the glass? What would be the point? And in any case, this can't be *the* glass. I mean, first thing you'd do if someone chucked themselves out of your window would be to replace the glass. Yes? Yes. Anybody can see that. And I can see the glass. I'm right up to it now. Looking out–where he must have looked. Out into the garden. And I can tell you this–it's a long, long way down. The scorched earth is just a dot. Even the concrete looks like you could miss it if you weren't concentrating on exactly where to throw yourself.

I want to touch the edge of the glass. To feel its sharpness. But I don't dare. Because all of a sudden I don't trust myself. I don't trust myself not to go too far. You know how it is when you stand on the edge of an underground platform and, just when you hear the train coming, you think, oh–I might just throw myself onto the tracks. And–although you don't, you can't stop the thought? Well, that's what I'm thinking. If I get any closer I might just do it. I might chuck myself out. So I step back. Just like you do on the underground platform. Behind the safety of the white line.

Only here there isn't a white line. There are only the ducks and the door. So I make for the door, and I'm running now and I'm not minding about the noise I'm making and I'm making plenty of noise, panting and whimpering and creaking and clattering, and sponge sinking and tile-shard skidding, down and down, right down to the door with the brick and through that to the stripped kitchen and finally back into the garden, where I take lungful after deep lungful of air.

And it's all so ordinary. It is bright. The sun is shining and there are birds singing. Twittering in the sky. At least I think it's ordinary until the slow motion starts. I see a comb in the grass and then I see all the grass as hair. And beyond that, thick ropes of ivy gripping a fallen tree take the shape of a monkey clinging to its mother's stomach. And even the discarded microwave becomes a casket, the condensation on the inside of the screen gathering into opalescent jewels joined by a thread of quicksilver where a snail has trailed.

It's as though the world has suddenly decided to let me in on some marvelous secret and is playing with me, gleeful, delighted. Or maybe it's me that's delighted. Me that's been to the top of Chance House and got away with it! I feel light, airy and full of energy. I could skip, I could dance. Well, I could if I had the coordination. As it is I'm just sort of wheeling about, dizzying my way towards the gasworks and my first lesson with the divine Miss Raynham.

"Watch it, you!"

I almost bump into some gentleman with a bulldog. I smile, I wave at him.

"Sorry!"

"Youth of today," he snarls.

But I'm spinning away. Me—Norbert No-Bottle, hero of Chance House! I waft across the main road, narrowly missing a double-decker bus. A white van comes to a halt with a screech of brakes, but I don't think it's to do with me. Because I'm already on the pavement, whirling through the gates of St. Michael and All Angels. Going via the churchyard is not as short a route to school as via the gasworks but it is more decorative. There are gravestones and flowers and bag ladies and surveillance cameras with notices that say whatever you do will be captured on film forever.

What I do for the cameras is—fall over. I don't think it's on account of a gravestone. I think it's just my feet getting tangled up in each other. Anyhow,

I crash to the ground. The two thousand pigeons that have made St. Michael and All Angels their home take to the air in a furious beat of wings. My mouth is full of mud and grass and something hard. Two hard things, in fact. Gravel, I think. I sit up and spit. But I can't see what I have in my palm because my glasses have gone missing in the fall. I scrabble about. I crawl on my hands and knees among the tombstones and then—hallelujah—my specs. I put them on. They are muddy but not broken. I open my palm. The things in there are small chips of white marble. One is streaked with blood, presumably from the inside of my cheek. They're the sort of chippings you put round flower containers in graveyards, and, as people get picky about things like this, I decide to replace them.

There is only one grave with similar chippings. I shuffle back to it and deposit my offerings round a vase of fresh daffodils. Then I squint up to see on whose grave I fell.

The headstone is gray marble and the black words engraved there are: Our beloved son aged 12 years. The date is 1967 and the name of the child is David Sorrel.

8

I'm fine in school. Trust me. I'm cool. You'd never know I wasn't having an ordinary day. I take an enormous interest in Pythagoras (Mr. Brand), the bubonic plague (Mrs. Greene) and the correct use of quotation marks (Miss Raynham). This is what I learn: Pythagoras was a Greek mathematician who invented some theory about right-angled triangles and didn't eat beans because he thought they had souls; the plague, contrary to popular belief, was not carried by rats but by the fleas who lived on the rats; and quotation marks are the punctuation marks that you use to indicate speech in text.

Wesley says: "Quotation marks look a bit like beans, don't they Miss Raynham? Do you think they could have souls?"

"Wesley Parr," says Miss Raynham, "you are a buffoon."

"High praise," says Niker.

I go with the flow. I smile, put my hand up, take notes, whatever's required. I simply don't have the time to think about anything else. Or anyone else. Certainly not David Sorrel.

At lunch I'm really normal. Chatting and grinning. Even though it's sausage casserole, which I hate.

"Are you auditioning for the wide-mouth frog joke?" Niker asks.

Which just leaves Friday afternoon PE. I'm looking forward to it. Not, you understand, because I'm any good at soccer. I'm not. In fact, I'm completely hopeless at soccer. The only time I touch the ball is when someone mis-hits it and it ricochets off me by mistake. I did save a goal once, though. But only, I think, because Niker deliberately aimed the ball at my head. And, as we know, he's good with his aim, Niker.

Anyway, the reason I'm looking forward to gym is because I really have to concentrate when I'm on the field; firstly, to keep my glasses on my nose, and secondly, not to fall over Niker's feet. He likes to trip me.

He even does it when we're on the same side. I think his theory is that it doesn't much matter to the flow of play whether I'm standing upright or lying flat on my face. Anyhow, it's a bit of a blow when Miss Raynham comes into the cloakroom after lunch and announces: "No need to change, children. PE is off."

"What!"

"Mr. Burke has been taken ill and, in view of the rain . . ."

There are wails and moans. I'm one of the wailers. Wesley looks out of the window.

"It's only spitting. Mr. Burke makes us play when it's torrential."

"*Nil desperandum,* Mr. Parr," says Miss Raynham. "We are, despite everything, going to have a most entrancing afternoon. Follow me, please."

We follow her. I hope we are making for the gymnasium. Basketball is as much of a trial for me as soccer, and therefore requires as much concentration. And the floor is harder, if you fall on it. Which I do. But no—Miss Raynham leads us to the art room.

"Find your places, everyone. Now—as you know, some children have been attending the Mayfield Rest Home. And some very interesting artworks are beginning to emerge from the project, so—"

"No."

"What did you say, Robert?"

"No. No."

"You don't even know what I'm going to ask, Robert."

But I do. She's going to ask us to do show-and-tell. Miss Raynham is going to ask us to "share" our experiences of Mayfield. She's going to make me speak about Edith Sorrel. And if I speak about Edith I'm going to speak about Chance House and then . . .

"I feel sick."

Weasel bangs his fist on the art bench. "Fleas." He makes a show of picking something up between finger and thumb. "Do you think the fleas have got him, Miss Raynham?"

"Wesley Parr. Stand out."

"But Miss Raynham, look at him." Weasel points at me. "He doesn't look too good, does he?"

"He always looks like that," says Niker.

"No, seriously. Pasty face. Boils. Sick. It could be the Black Death, couldn't it? I mean who's to say?"

"Wesley Parr—stand out!"

Weasel stands up.

"Over there."

Weasel moves slowly if jauntily toward the basins. Miss Raynham waits.

"Right. Thank you, Wesley."

"Miss Raynham . . ." Kate has her hand up.

"What is it now?"

"I don't think Robert does look very well."

"Thank you, Miss Nightingale." Miss Raynham moves swiftly to my side and sticks a nail under my chin. "Florence is concerned about you," she says.

"I don't want to talk about Chance House," I say.

"That's lucky," says Miss Raynham, removing her finger so fast my head falls on the desk. "Because no one's asking you to." She beams. "Now, if we could proceed . . ." She makes her way to the back of the classroom and fingers some pieces of paper on the map drawers. "What have we here?" She turns a piece of paper over. "Oh yes, Kate. Kate Barber, perhaps you'd like to start? Tell us a bit about your Elder and what you're doing with her."

"Him," says Kate, getting up and taking the paper.

"Front of the class, now."

Kate goes and stands by Mrs. Simpson's desk. She looks uncomfortable.

"I'm not asking you to declaim Shakespeare, just tell us a little about your Elder and the work you're making together. You could start perhaps with the man's name."

"Albert," says Kate.

"Good. Now tell us something about him."

"Well, he's eighty-two and he left school at thirteen."

"Lucky," says Niker.

"Then he earned sixpence a day working first in the sawmills and then 'on the building.' He clocked on at half past six in the morning and finished at six at night, with half an hour off for breakfast and an hour for lunch."

"Not so lucky, then, perhaps," says Miss Raynham, meaningfully.

"And for the artwork we're collecting songs. Because Albert really likes singing. And you know the story Catherine told, about the Prince who wouldn't speak? Well, Albert's idea is that you can sometimes sing things you can't speak. So if he was trying to break the spell, he might sing to the Prince. And maybe the Prince would sing back."

"Good. Good. Thank you, Kate. Can you show us the work?"

"Well, I can't sing it, but this is one of Albert's favorites." From the paper she recites:

> *"The first time I met you, my darling,*
> *Your cheeks were as red as a rose.*
> *But now they're old and faded,*
> *They're as white as the whitest of rose.*
> *Still I love the white rose in its splendor,*
> *I love the white rose in its bloom.*
> *I love that rose, the sweetest that grows,*
> *It's the rose that reminds me of you."*

She holds up the paper for us to see. The poem is written in black ink on a square of gray. Around the edge of the picture are sketches of flowers, which have yet to be painted.

"Why have you drawn it on a gravestone?" asks Niker.

"It's not a gravestone. It's a paving stone. Albert's idea of the path, remember?"

"Well, I think it's wonderful," says Miss Raynham. "Thank you very much, Kate."

"Can I do it now?" asks a voice from the basin.

"If you can be sensible, Wesley. Can you be sensible, Wesley?"

"Yes, Miss Raynham."

Wesley goes to the back of the class and collects some red, orange, yellow and black strips of paper.

"Is yours a paving stone, too, Wesley?" asks Niker.

"Nope. Mine's a fire." Wesley makes his way to the front and perches himself on the corner of Mrs. Simpson's desk. "Gotta warm dat dere princie up. Dat's what Dulcie and me reckons."

"Dulcie and I," says Miss Raynham.

"Dulcie and I," repeats Wesley, "Dulcie and I have been discussing potatoes. Dulcie is seventy-six. When she was my age she used to come home from school at twelve o'clock, boil some potatoes, eat them and return to school by one-thirty."

"And what have you learned from that, Wesley?"

"That they didn't have chips in those days, Miss Raynham. And," he adds quickly as he sees her finger begin to wag, "that they had more responsibility."

"Oh?"

"Yes. As well as lighting the gas, Dulcie got to peel the potatoes with a very sharp knife and drain boiling water. On top of that—it was her job to light the parlor fire every morning. Get the coal in, lay the fire and light it. Me—my mum doesn't even let me have a match."

"Really," says Miss Raynham.

"So these are some flames Dulcie and I have painted. This one"—he indicates an orange strip—"this one says 'We didn't come to no harm.'"

"Any harm," says Miss Raynham.

"'No harm,'" says Wesley. "That's what Dulcie said." He mimics: "'You lot is babied today. We didn't come to no harm.'"

"I see," says Miss Raynham. "The verbatim report."

"What?"

"Carry on, Wesley. You interest me."

"And this one"—Wesley waves a red flame—"says 'No Irish. No Blacks.'" He grins.

Did I mention that Wesley's black? Or rather, he's the color of coffee with milk in, on account of his mum being black and his dad white. Miss Raynham is always trying to get Wesley to talk about What It

Means to Be Black in Today's Society. And Wesley is always telling Miss Raynham that He Hasn't the Faintest Idea.

"That's the good news," continues Wesley.

"The good news?" inquires Miss Raynham.

"Yeah. In Dulcie's day, you see, they didn't like renting to Irish people or blacks. So they stuck the 'No Irish, No Blacks' notice in the window of their houses. To save embarrassment."

"Right."

"But now," says Wesley triumphantly, "it's different. There's progress. People rent to the Irish, don't they?"

"But not to black people, is that what you're saying, Wesley?"

"I haven't the faintest idea, Miss Raynham."

"How does any of this help the Prince?" says Niker.

"Knowledge," says Wesley, tapping his nose, "is a very wonderful t'ing, Jonathan."

"Thank you very much, Wesley. I think we'll move on now. Jonathan, how about you taking up the baton?"

Niker collects what looks like two blank sheets of paper and makes his way to the front. He begins to talk, and as he talks he walks, pacing slowly in front of the desk, pausing occasionally for dramatic effect.

"My Elder is called Mavis. I do not know how old she is because she does not know how old she is. As well as forgetting her birth date she seems to have forgotten almost every other thing that has ever happened to her. If you ask her about her past, she says 'I'm going to Abingdon.' If you ask her about the future, she asks you when tea is. In fact, I think 'When's tea?' was the first sensible thing Mavis said to me. But after she'd said it six times in a row, it suddenly didn't seem quite so sensible anymore. In fact, it seemed mad. And—"

"Is there a point to this, Jonathan?"

"The point, Miss Raynham, is get on with your life while you can. That's what I'd tell the Prince. Stop mucking about and get on with it. Before it's too late."

"Oh," says Miss Raynham, impressed despite herself. "Well—let's see the pictures then."

Niker holds up the first piece of paper. It's a pencil portrait of Mavis as a chicken. But it's not a grotesque caricature, it's a detailed, accurate and quite fond picture of Mavis. It shows her with her head on one side and a bewildered but charming chicken look in her eyes. On the second sheet of paper, he has drawn Mavis as an angel. In this picture she is much younger, in her twenties. The chicken wings are soft, downy, fledgling angel wings and her look is one of serenity and hope. Once again it is piercingly accurate.

"I wish I could draw like that," says Kate, voicing the class's thought.

Miss Raynham, who's never seen Mavis so doesn't know how accurate the representation is, nevertheless appreciates the quality of the drawing.

"Jonathan," she says sadly, "you're a wasted talent."

"Thank you," says Niker.

Then it happens. Miss Raynham turns to me.

"Robert," she says, "if you'd do us the honor."

Niker resumes his seat. I don't move from mine.

"If you'd like to find the artwork . . ."

But that's the problem. Or one of them. While the others have been busy cutting and sticking, I have been talking to people a lot madder than Mavis. I've been talking to a man who may or may not be married to a woman who may or may not remember some dreadful thing that happened to a boy who may or may not have been her son. And instead of having a nice piece of paper with a drawing on, I have a cut on the inside of my cheek from eating gravel from a grave and the distinct taste of strawberry jam in my mouth when I think about star-shaped holes in windows.

"Robert," prompts Miss Raynham, "could you speed up a little, do you think?"

Believe me, I've been thinking very fast the whole of this lesson. I have an impressive array of wisdoms to share with the class. I have prepared a speech about selective memory and about being able to do anything you want, if you want to enough (including flying) and about—

"Robert!" yells Miss Raynham. "Front of the class. Now!"

I get up. I go to the front of the class. I stand there. My mouth is opening and closing like a fish's.

"Yes, Robert. And?"

"Sad," says Niker.

"Name?" says Miss Raynham.

"Robert."

"Not your name, Robert. I am aware of your name. Robert. The name of your Elder."

"Miss Sorrel. Mrs. Sorrel."

"Well, which?"

"Edith."

"Right. Edith."

"I haven't done a drawing."

"Well, don't tell us what you haven't done, Robert. Tell us what you have done."

"I've been to the Top-Floor Flat, Chance House, twenty-six St. Aubyns."

"Liar," says Niker.

"I had to go. She asked me."

"Who? What are you talking about?"

"Edith. She asked me. She said it was there. Her

wisdom. But it isn't. There's nothing there. It's derelict."

Miss Raynham walks to the front of the class and puts a sweaty hand on my forehead. Or maybe it's my forehead that's sweaty.

"Are you still feeling sick?" she asks.

"No. Yes."

Wesley swipes the desk. "These fleas," he says.

I cough. Miss Raynham delves into her pocket and produces a large, folded cotton handkerchief. I put it to my mouth.

"Gross," says Niker.

He thinks I'm spitting and that gives me an idea. I chew the inside of my cheek and then I do spit. Blood goes onto the handkerchief. Feebly I present the bloodied rag to Miss Raynham.

"Oh, Robert, dear child. Come with me." And this giant, suddenly motherly woman conducts me out of the art room and along the corridor, her arm around my shoulder, her bosom wobbling against my face.

"Temporary sickroom," she says, opening the door of the staff room. It smells of stale perfume and stale smoke.

"Sit." She indicates a green, soggy-looking arm-chair. "I'll phone the nurse."

But I don't want to sit. In fact I can't sit. Because something inside me is heaving. I bend double, I convulse; then, without warning, my body straightens like a whip, and something red and evil vomits out of my throat. It lands on Miss Raynham's large bosom. It spatters her. I think it's sausage casserole.

"Oh dear," says Miss Raynham, rather mildly. "Oh dear, dear, dear."

9

"Sick?" *inquires my* mother.

As it is the end of the day, Miss Raynham has dispensed with the idea of the school nurse and phoned the hospital. She has extracted my mother from the ward of seriously sick patients she's paid to care for and put me on the end of the line to explain myself.

"I'm fine," I say. "It's nothing."

"I'll come if you need me," says Mum.

"It's OK. I said I'm fine."

"Love you," Mum says.

"Yes," I reply, and put the phone down.

"Well?"

"She can't come." Miss Raynham raises an eyebrow. "There's been an emergency."

"I see," says Miss Raynham. She pats her bosom. The fluffy gray sweater on which the sausage casserole landed has been tied into a plastic bag. The seepage on the red blouse beneath has been wiped with water and tissues. There are flecks of white on the damp stain. Miss Raynham rolls one under a nail. "Well, I suppose that's that."

"Yes," I say, and try a smile.

She opens her mouth, she's about to begin again and then the bell goes. There's an immediate and deafening end-of-day clamor. Feet skid, book bags flump, kids roar and holler.

Miss Raynham opens the staff room door. "A little less noise, there," she says.

I edge out behind her. "Can I go now? Please?"

I start off down the corridor toward the cloakroom. She follows me.

"A little less noise, there, I said," she bawls.

There's a disgruntled, scuffling silence.

"I think I ought to accompany you home," Miss Raynham announces suddenly, in front of everyone.

"No!" I cry. "Thank you. I'm fine now. I really am."

Now there's a real silence.

"I'll go with him," says a voice. "I live that way."

It's Kate and she doesn't. In fact, although we both

live within five minutes' walk of the school, her route home lies in precisely the opposite direction from mine.

A dark head appears above the pegs to my right. "You heard him," says Niker. "He doesn't need the company. He's fine. Really fine."

"A kind offer, nevertheless," says Miss Raynham, briskly. "What do you say, Robert?"

"Erm . . ." I could be feeling sick again. "Erm . . ."

"That's settled then. Thank you very much, Kate. Take a Good Conduct Plus."

"Thank you, Miss Raynham."

Miss Raynham leaves.

"What's happened to your own mum, Norbie?" asks Niker. "She abandoned you as well, has she?"

"Shut up, Niker."

"First your dad walks out. And now your mum's—"

"I said *Shut up*, Niker."

Niker smiles, pulls an empty crisp bag from his pocket and hands it to Kate.

"What's that for?" she asks.

"Sick bag," he says.

"I told you," I say, "I'm not going to be sick again."

"Yeah," says Niker. "But Kate might be. After walking home with you."

Kate balls the crisp packet. "Come on," she says to me. "Let's go."

We go. I turn right out of the school gate.

Kate pauses. "Isn't it quicker that way?" she asks. "Through the Dog Leg?"

"Uh—yes," I say. "But I want to show you something. Do you mind?"

"What?" she asks.

"Just something," I say. "Something I . . . found."

She looks at her watch.

"Are you in a hurry?"

"No," she says. "S'pose not."

"Thanks," I say.

She shrugs.

"No, I mean it. Thanks. Thanks a lot."

And then she smiles and that dimple comes. Just for me. And of course I had no intention of showing her David Sorrel's grave, no intention of going back to look at it myself. But that smile almost makes it seem like a good idea. A great idea.

The graveyard is barely twenty-five meters from the school gate, just along past the fenced playing field, and then first right. Not much time to wind yourself into a frenzy but this is what happens: I wind myself into a frenzy. It's all going too well, isn't it? So suddenly I think there will be no white marble chippings, no fresh daffodils. No headstone of David Sorrel, aged 12. It will all have been my own sick (and I have been sick) imagination. And I'll be left wandering round the graveyard showing Kate the pigeons.

We arrive.

"Yes?" says Kate.

I scan the graves, take a breath, point.

"A pigeon?" says Kate.

There are about a hundred pigeons perched on gravestones. I lower my finger. Beneath a particularly fat white bird is the headstone of our beloved son, David Sorrel, aged 12.

Kate follows the line of my finger. "Oh," she says. And then again, as she gets closer, "Oh, oh, Robert." She squats by the grave, but quietly. The pigeon remains where he is, looking at her. She stretches out a hand, can't stop herself touching the sharply indented number 12. Then her hand falls. "They're fresh," she says of the daffodils. "Somebody's put fresh flowers here."

"Ernest Sorrel," I say.

She turns a quizzical face upward.

"Mrs. Sorrel's husband. It can't be Edith herself. She's too ill to leave the home."

"Are you sure this really is—was—their child?"

I want to shrug, I want not to know. But I say: "Yes. Sure."

Kate stands up. "He'd have been old now. Over forty."

"And have children of his own maybe. Grandchildren for Mrs. Sorrel."

Standing, Kate and I are about the same height. Her eyes level with mine. "Did Mrs. Sorrel really ask you to go to Chance House?"

"Yes."

"And?"

"And I went."

"'O villain, villain, smiling, damned villain!'" An apparition erupts from behind the tomb of Claude Mosen, aged 86. It grins insanely. It waves its arms. Pigeons scatter. "I am the ghost of Claudie Mosen! Come from the foul and fetid beyond to warn of the fell fibs of Norbert No-Brain, otherwise known as Norbert No-Bottle, No-Chance, No–"

"Don't you ever give up?" says Kate.

Niker vaults over the tomb and lands like a cat at her feet.

"Never," he says, straightening up and grinning. "First rule of chivalry–a man of honor is duty bound to challenge a lie. To listen to a lie and remain silent is, my lady, tantamount to–"

"Yes, yes," says Kate. "Whatever."

"OK," says Niker. "Have it your way. Norbert No-Bottle could no more find the courage to go to the top of Chance House than he could be relied on to jump out of the window when he got there." He laughs. "More's the pity." Then he turns to me. "Am I right or am I right?"

"You're wrong," I say. And even though it's the truth it frightens me to say it. I have never challenged Niker so directly before. And certainly not in front of someone else.

"I see." Niker's not laughing now. He's by my side, jerking his face into mine. "Prove it," he says. "Chum."

"The window of the top room's broken," I say quickly. "In the shape of a star."

"The room that looks over the back garden, you mean?"

"Yes."

"Brilliant." Niker relaxes. "Take top grades in sleuthing, Norbie."

"What?" says Kate.

"Well, Your Honor," says Niker. "The defendant, Mr. N for Norbert No-Brain, asserts he's been to the top of Chance House. The rather more intelligent prosecuting counsel—Mr. J for Jugular Niker—submits that Norbert's been into the garden, looked up at the Top-Floor Flat, noticed—from the outside—the broken window—and bingo! Two plus two equals three."

"There's wallpaper," I say.

"Really," says Niker. "And a floor, no doubt."

"It's got ducks on."

"Would that be the wallpaper or the floor, Norbie?"

"The wallpaper! A mother duck and her three ducklings."

"Not flying pigs then?"

"Ducks."

"Flying ducks?"

I turn to Kate. "You believe me, don't you?"

Kate's head swings slowly between me and Niker.

"A contest," says Niker, delighted. "The goddess chooses. A flower for the hero who's telling the truth." He whips a daffodil from the vase on David Sorrel's grave.

"You can't do that," says Kate.

"I just have," says Niker.

"It's sacrilege," says Kate.

"It's a daffodil," says Niker.

Kate snatches the flower from him and jams it back into the pot, breaking its stem.

"Choose," says Niker. "Choose!"

"This is stupid."

"Choose. You have to choose!"

"Right," says Kate, furiously. "Here's the plan. You go to that room, Johnny, and you check it out. Go right to the top and then you'll see for yourself if there are or aren't any ducks, won't you!"

"Ha," says Niker. "Queen Solomon herself." He gives me a sidelong glance. "I think I will go. In fact I think I'll take a sleeping bag and spend the night there. All in the dark, Norbie. Whoo . . . Whoo . . ." He makes ghost noises. "Only"—he contrives to look confused—"only how will you know I've really done it? How could I proo-oove it to you, Norbie? Mm. Tricky." He sucks the tips of his fingers. "I know." He grabs me round the neck. "You'll have to come too. You and me alone in the Top-Floor Flat, Chance House. How about it, Norbie?"

"I . . . I . . ."

"You can't be scared, Norbie. Because you've already been there, haven't you? So you know there's nothing in that room"—his voice drops to a whisper—"but . . . *ducks!*"

Now this is what's happening. I am shaking from head to foot. Not because Niker's got his hands round my throat and is screaming *"ducks"* in my ear but because if there's one thing in the world I don't want to do, it's spend a night alone in the Top-Floor Flat, Chance House. I cannot imagine anything more horrible. Except—perhaps—spending the night in the Top-Floor Flat, Chance House, with Jonathan Niker.

"No . . . ," I say. "No, Niker. Please . . . I couldn't."

"Why's that, Norbie? Is it because there are no *ducks* in that room after all?" He winks at Kate.

"There are ducks." It's quite difficult to speak when someone has their hands round your throat, so I'm sort of gasping really. "And people."

"People, eh?"

"A brick," I gasp. "It moves."

"A moving brick, Norbie? Sort of jumps out of its wall and moves around among the ducks, does it?"

"Floor."

"Oh, on the floor. A brick on the floor. Right."

"And people."

"Yeah, you said that. And do you know who one of them is, moving between the bricks and ducks, Norbie? I think it might be that boy who died, don't you? The strawberry jam one? Wandering about with his little ghostie feet slep-slepping on the jam. Whaddya think, Norbert?"

I can't speak now. Either because I just can't or because Niker has finally succeeded in squeezing all the air from my throat.

"I think you should go, Robert," says Kate. She smiles. The dimple is blurred.

Niker lets me go and my head nods as it hits the ground.

"Tomorrow night then," says Niker. "Sleeping bags at dusk. Can't wait." He picks up his schoolbag from behind Claude Mosen's tomb and slouches off. But he's only gone a few feet when he wheels round: "If you don't show, Norbert, I'll kill you."

I'm still on my knees, trying to get some air back into my lungs.

"And if *you* don't show," Kate says to Niker, "then no doubt *he'll* kill *you*."

Niker whistles. "Scary!" Then he's gone.

I still haven't moved.

Kate looks down at me. "You don't have to be so pathetic," she says.

"What?"

"Oh, never mind." She extends a hand and pulls me roughly to my feet. And then she says: "He's only talk, Niker."

"Did you ever hear about the Grape Incident?" I ask.

"No."

"That wasn't just talk," I say.

"Oh?"

"I . . . I'll . . . I'll tell you another time."

"Oh, Robert."

We walk the rest of the way home in silence. A silence that makes me feel both stupid and miserable. When we get to my back gate, I want to invite her in. But of course I don't and even if I did, I know she wouldn't accept.

"Bye," I say.

"Bye, Robert," she says. I watch her going. She sets off through the Dog Leg without a backward glance. I unchain, unbolt and unlock my way into the house.

"I can see you," I yell into the sitting room. Then I

just give up. If there were anyone in the house waiting to hit me over the head with a vase, then, the way things are, they'd be doing me a favor. I sit down on the floor. My only hope is, I suppose, that Mum will see through it. That she won't let me go. That she'll phone up Mrs. Niker and tell her that it's all completely ridiculous. It'll mean I'll get called chicken and be beaten up at school on Monday, which won't be great, but, on balance, it will be better than being pushed out of a fourth-floor window.

I don't know how long I sit on the floor but I'm still there when Mum comes home.

"Robert? Robert?" Mum switches on the light. "Hey—what you doing in the dark?"

"Practicing."

"What?"

"Thinking. Just thinking."

"You OK?"

"Yes."

"Sure? Not sick anymore?"

"Not sick anymore."

"Is it to do with your dad? Because he's not coming when he promised?"

"No."

"We'll do something nice. We'll do something nice anyway tomorrow night. What would you like to do, Robert? Just say."

"Niker's invited me over."

"Oh."

"Wants me to bring a sleeping bag. Sleepover. You know."

"And do you want to go?"

"Yes. Course. Why wouldn't I?"

"All right. Fine." She kneels down, put her arms around me. "I'm really pleased." She chucks me under the chin. "It'll be great. Yes? Looking forward to it?"

"Can't wait," I say.

10

Niker rings to say: Forget dusk. We'll meet at Chance House at 8 P.M. Nice and dark, eh?

"Fine," I say. But it's not fine. Not just because of the dark—though that's bad enough, but because if I don't leave till just before eight, Mum will get suspicious. She'll start saying stuff like: "What sort of parent invites a boy round for the night but isn't prepared to give him supper?" And then I'll have to think of an answer which isn't quite the truth but isn't exactly a lie either. And things will get difficult. So I pack my backpack at 6 P.M. and announce: "Niker rang."

"Yes?"

"His mum's taking us to supper at Marrocco's."

"Oh–that's nice."

"So I'll walk. Meet them there. Is that OK?"

"Of course." Everyone knows Marrocco's. It's a seafront cafe owned by a gregarious, generous Italian couple. It's renowned for its ice cream. Its food. Its welcome. A family place. Safe and warm. A good place to while away time. And I will have supper there. Well, chips anyway. I've got a little money. So I'm not lying. Not really.

She kisses the top of my head. "God bless," she says.

She doesn't say that very often. In fact the last time she said "God bless" was before she went out to dinner with Dad to discuss their separation. When they returned that night, we were a one-parent family.

"Bye," I say.

"Sure you don't want me to walk with you?"

"Mum . . ."

"Just asking." She smiles and waves me into the night.

It's dark but of course there are streetlights. Warm lozenges of orange, the color of hard candy. I wish I could pluck them from their lampposts, pop them in my pocket for later, for just in case. Do streetlamps go off–or are they ablaze all hours of the night? I haven't thought about that before. Haven't had to. What about the stars? I stop walking, look up. It's cold and clear. So there are stars. A whole heaven of them. That has to be a good omen.

It gets windier as you approach the seafront. I pull my collar up about my neck. I'm wearing my thick waterproof jacket with the rain-colored quilting inside. I don't often wear it, because it's rather old-fashioned. "Is it your granddad's?" Weasel asked when I wore it to school once. But it's the warmest jacket I have and if I'm going to be shivering, I don't want it to be from the cold.

I could take St. Aubyns and then St. Aubyns South onto the Esplanade. But of course I don't. I choose Medina Villas and then Medina Terrace. I tell myself it's quicker, but it isn't. It's just less frightening. As soon as you turn the corner from Medina into the Esplanade you can see Marrocco's. I turn the corner. There are no lights on at the cafe and no menu board outside.

Marrocco's is shut.

But Marrocco's being shut is not part of my plan, so I keep on walking. I stride purposefully along the seafront as if, if I just keep going, the Italians will suddenly appear, unlock the door and start frying chips. They don't. I arrive at the door and press my nose to the glass. My safe haven is bolted and dark. Like many seafront places they close at dusk in the winter. There just isn't the business to justify staying open any longer. I've lived in this town long enough to know that. Need makes you forget things, I guess. Selective memory again.

I stand back from the cafe and look up at the second-floor windows. What am I expecting now? That if I chuck a few pebbles up at the windows the family will come down and rescue me?

I chuck a few pebbles. But not at the windows—at the beach. Fat, sea-smoothed, flint pebbles lifted onto the promenade by the wind. I thunk them back where they belong. Thunk. Thunk. Thunk. What am I going to do now? I lob a huge rock, one that looks too big to have been wind-lifted, onto the beach. It bounces. Fine. I'll go somewhere else. Who cares about Marrocco's anyhow? There are any number of places to get chips along the Kingsway. I'll just stop at the first place I come to.

The first place I come to is Vinney's. It's not a pleasant little cafe with red-and-white-checkered tablecloths and a smiling proprietor. It's a seedy fish-and-chip shop with a cracked lino floor and chipped Formica on the one table inside. It's difficult to know which is greasier, the deep-fat fryer or the man standing behind it.

"Yeah?" the deep-fat man says to me. There are little bubbles of sweat on his forehead.

"Chips, please," I say.

"Small? Large?"

"Do you have medium?"

"If we'd have had medium, I'd of said, wouldn't I?"

"Large, then. Thank you." I don't want to appear mean, or like I can't afford it.

He shovels chips into a bag. "Eat now?"

"Yes."

"Salt? Vinegar?"

"Please." He shakes and splashes. Then he slaps another couple of sheets of paper around the bag. "One pound thirty."

On the board behind him it says large chips are £1.20. But Deep-Fat doesn't look like the type of man you argue with so I pay up.

Gingerly, I loosen the chip paper. The chips are pale and fat. Squarish slugs of potato lolling on each other. I turn one over between finger and thumb. It's limp, lukewarm and has a slightly gray tinge.

"Do you have tomato ketchup?" I ask.

"Ketchup's extra," says Deep-Fat.

"I'll give it a miss then," I say. Even I have my limits.

"Suit yerself."

I sit. I stir the chips. I push them under the flaps of paper. I observe how the grease turns the paper transparent. I lick a couple of grains of salt from my fingertips, but I don't eat the chips. I know I should eat the chips. Partly because I've paid for them, partly because I know there isn't going to be a McDonald's on the top floor of Chance House and partly because I'm ravenously hungry. But I can't eat. Just looking at these chips closes up my gullet. Just smelling them. So I sit and I sit and I stir. Deep-Fat watches me.

"What's up wiv yer?" he asks finally.

"Nothing."

"You got a problem with them chips?"

"No."

"Looks like yer have."

"Last supper syndrome," I say.

"You what?"

"When you go to the electric chair," I say, "you get a last request. A last meal. You can have anything you want. In America they always order chips. Hamburger and chips. But what happens when the food comes? Do you think they can eat it? I mean, just half an hour before they make that final trip. The one to the buzz buzz chair. Good night, world. I mean, would you have any appetite, if it was you?" I'm saying this, but this is what I'm thinking: Suppose it was your last meal and they sent you rubbish chips. I mean, would you think, Oh well, it doesn't really matter because I'll be cinders in half an hour anyway, or would it make you mad? Your very last wish on earth thwarted by some lousy cook? Would you jump and scream and demand a stay of execution until you got decent chips?

"You cheeking me?"

"No," I say.

"You are. You cheeky little blighter."

He comes out from behind the counter bearing a dripping red, squeezy bottle of ketchup.

"You give me sauce," he says, "and I'll give you sauce!" He lunges at me, squooshing ketchup over my chips. Great, sloppy puddles of red sauce, which look like regurgitated sausage casserole, or strawberry jam, or plain, old-fashioned blood.

"Oh no," I cry. "Please–"

"Oh yes," he replies, emphatically. "Oh yes! Here yer go! On the house!" He doesn't stop squeezing until my plate is a lake of red. Then he wipes his brow with his sleeve, takes a fat satisfied breath and points the bottle at me. "Now, get out of here, you little creep."

I don't need telling twice. I grab for my jacket, fumble and drop it. As I bend over to get it, I hear the burp of the sauce bottle. There's a wet flimp on my neck, my hair. The back of my sweatshirt. "You understand English?" he yells. "I said, scram! Beat it!"

Don't worry. I scram. I beat it. But I do have the foresight to grab a couple of napkins in transit.

"You filthy little thief," he screams. "I'll get the police on you."

But I'm already across the Kingsway and into Vallance Gardens. I don't stop for at least two hundred yards, not until I'm out of breath and convinced he's not following me. Then I wipe my hair and neck with the napkins but I can't reach the muck on my back. So I position myself in the dark space between two garages and take off my top. It's a light blue sweatshirt and the ketchup makes it look like I've been shot in the back. I do my best with the remaining napkins, only they're the thin, cheap sort that don't really absorb anything, so I just end up smearing the sauce. But it's too cold to be fussy, so I put the top back on. If anyone were to look now they'd have to assume I recently stepped on a land mine. Thank goodness for my jacket. I put that on too and jump up and down. As some sensation returns to my freezing body I wonder this: are there murderees in the same way as there are murderers? I mean, for every person who wants to kill someone is there also someone just asking to be killed? Is there a victim type? Someone who has a large sign on their head saying: Hey, why don't you just kick me? Because sometimes, I think that's what must be written on my forehead. In really big letters. A neon sign that everyone can see but me: Hey, take a look at Robert Nobel, he's fair game, take a potshot at him. Maybe being a victim is genetic. Maybe Mum has the sign too and that's why Dad chucked dishes.

I stop jumping. There's no way Deep-Fat would have squirted Niker with tomato sauce.

It's then that I look at my watch. It's five to eight. I don't believe it! After all this time-wasting, I'm going to be late. I start running, but I'm not sure why. Is it normal for condemned men to run to their executions? I mean, what's the hurry? The fact that Niker said he'd kill me if I wasn't there? What difference is that going to make?

I'm running so hard my glasses are steaming up. I arrive, panting, at 8:04. At first I think I can't see Niker because I can't see anything. Then I wipe my glasses and he still isn't there. Not at the front of the house anyway. Not on the steps. Not on the wall. I scan the street and notice, for the first time, how the lampposts here are the same as in the Dog Leg. Only bigger. Fluted, old-fashioned, green metal lampposts with the extended arm where you might hang a coat. Or sit. I half expect Niker to be sitting on the one closest to the house. But he isn't.

Can he have gone round the back already? I edge my way around the side of the house. It is much darker here, the pools of light from the street hardly penetrating at all. Beneath my feet the ground seems lumpy, humps of mud, tussocky grass. I don't remember the earth being so uneven before. But that was when I could see it. Something grabs at my leg and for some reason I think it's wire, even though I know it has to be the low branches of one of the overgrown bushes. I want to reach for the torch that's in my backpack but I don't. Because, although I want to see, I don't want to be seen. So I stumble on to the corner and turn into the wet, still garden. It's even darker here, no light at all from the street and only the smallest spill of yellow from a couple of lit windows in adjacent buildings. Where are the stars? I look up. The night has clouded over and the sky is now a haunting milky blue.

I listen for a sound that might be Niker. Though I'm not entirely sure what sort of sound Niker might be making in a dark garden all by himself. I hear the hum of a generator, a drip that could be guttering, the honk and swerve of cars and, rather nearer, the sound of my own breathing. I walk toward the kitchen, stepping suddenly from grass to concrete. My feet making a different noise here, hard and echoless.

What if Niker's already gone in? What if he's waiting in the house for me? Slowly, I tilt my head upward. He'd go to the room, of course. Stand at the broken window. Look out. Down.

Next thing I hear is a violent crash, the sound of falling and a scream. I wheel around.

"For Chrissake—who left that there?"

Niker has fallen over the microwave.

His body is spread-eagled in the dirt. As I look at him, I can't help thinking that if he'd fallen slightly to the left, he would have landed on the concrete.

"Are you just going to stand there gawping, or are you going to give me a hand?"

I give him a hand.

He pulls himself upright and claps off the worst of the dirt.

"Where's your backpack?" I ask.

"Backpack? What backpack?"

"Your one for . . . things."

"This isn't a hike in the Himalayas, Norbie. Just a little climb up some stairs in a house." He pauses. "Oh, right—don't tell me—you've brought cramping irons, an ice pick, a camping stove, some baked beans and a bar of soap."

"Crisps," I say. "And an apple."

"You are one serious Boy Scout, Norbert. Me—I just have the sleeping bag." He pauses. "Correction. Used to have the sleeping bag." He drops to his knees and begins scrabbling about in the grass. "Gotcha," he says after a minute or two. As he stands up he swings a small drawstring bag over his shoulder. "Now, let's get on with the job, shall we?"

He leads the way to the kitchen and ducks under the swinging mesh. The wind is strong enough to be grating the holly branch against the window over the nonexistent sink.

Scrape. Pause. Scrape.

"Shhh," I say to Niker.

"What?"

"Listen."

"To what?"

"That noise."

He listens.

Scrape. Pause. Scrape.

"Hear it?"

"Yes."

"What is it, Niker?" I want him to be as scared as I've been.

"Well, Norbert, I'd say it was the incredibly sinister sound of a tree branch scraping against a pane of glass. What would you say?"

But I'm not saying anything because I've just noticed the brick. Or rather the lack of brick. Of course, some of the dark shapes on the floor probably are bricks, but they don't look like my brick. The one that can be up against the door. But isn't. Which means either no one's been in the house since I was here last or—someone's in the house right now.

"Brick," I say.

"Don't start," says Niker. He kicks his way across the rubble and holds opens the door to the inner house. "After you."

I pick my way slowly across the room, climb the step and then stop. I don't want to be first into the corridor. Not just because of what might lie ahead but because of what will definitely lie behind. Niker. I don't want to have my back to him.

"Can we speed things up a bit here, Norbie?" There's a shove at the base of my spine and then I'm in the corridor. He is quickly in behind me and the door swings shut. I think he will push me again. But he doesn't. We are both held by the quality of the dark. It's like someone's thrown black paint in our eyes. I feel I ought to be able to rub it away, but I can't.

After a moment Niker says: "You got anything useful in that bag of yours?"

"Like what?"

"Like a torch, for instance?"

"Yes. Yes! I have."

I unbuckle the backpack and dip in my hand. Sleeping bag, crisp packet, apple, crisp packet, bottle of Evian water, penknife, crisp packet again. What if the torch never made it? Ridiculous. Crisp packet, apple, crisp packet. What if I left the torch on the bed? Packed everything else, but forgot the torch? I begin to scrabble. Crisps. Don't panic. Of course it's here, I can feel the weight of it. Although the weight could be the bottle of water. It's Dad's torch, the sealed black rubber one he used to keep in the car. Mum laughed at him, called it the Raincoat Torch, offered to buy it matching boots.

"Norbert . . ."

"Yes . . . yes . . . Got it!"

"Give it here."

Niker almost snatches the torch from me.

"Yeuch—what do you call this?"

"Car torch."

"Rubber nightstick more like." I can sense him turning it, searching for the 'On' button.

"It's waterproof."

"Ideal," says Niker. "Ah!" He locates the button. The beam is pale and insubstantial. He points the torch at the floor and then the ceiling. The beam barely reaches. "Does it have any setting other than dim? No, don't bother to answer that, Norbert."

Now he has the torch, Niker takes the lead. Quietly, I follow.

"What's that?"

He's found the gap between the floor and the skirting board. The torchlight flickers over the filing cabinets, the desk, the lampshades, the sink.

"Basement," I say.

"Basement!" scoffs Niker. "Den, more like. Problem with you, Norbert, is you have no imagination."

Problem with me is I have too much imagination. We are coming to the entrance hall, the one with the sledgehammered terra-cotta tiles. And I can hear that creak again. The wooden-gallows sound.

Creak. Cre-eak.

I look at Niker. He's got the torch low on the tiles. Can't he hear the creak?

"Jeez," says Niker. "Who's done this?" He picks up a broken tile and runs his finger down the edge. "Sharp as a knife, this. You could kill someone with one of these. Death by tile." As he stands up, I see him slip the shard into his pocket.

Creak. Creak.

Now he hears it. He turns toward the sound, faces the stairs, points the torch. But the beam doesn't quite reach.

"Did—"

"Shhh!" He extends his arm as if that will make the beam reach the bottom tread. It doesn't. And in any case the light is faltering, tremoring between dim and very dim.

Creak. Crea-ak.

"What is it?"

"It's the sound of the house," I say.

"Houses don't make sounds," Niker says.

"This one does."

He thrusts the torch into my face. I don't know whether he's looking for knowledge or fear. Niker would make a good interrogator. But not with this light. It's weakening by the minute. The moment. And Niker knows it, which is why he has it shining at me and not the stairs now because the beam does, just, reach my face. And he is pretending—as I am—that the batteries are not fading when they clearly are fading. The light wavers, it flickers, off, on, off, on. And then off. Off. No light at all. Not hazy. Not gloomy. But pitch black. I cannot see Niker. He cannot see me.

There's an appalled silence and then he yells: "You jerk! You stupid, idiotic, brainless jerk!" I hear him wrestling with the torch, pulling and pushing and tearing, as if he could bring it back to life by throttling it. "You're a moron," he continues. "An imbecile. A halfwit. A quarterwit. A drongo. How could you bring a torch with dud batteries, you, you . . . *gerbil*!"

"You," I mention, "didn't bring a torch at all."

He lunges toward my voice. I feel the force of his body as wind moving. But he never arrives. He catches a foot on one of the loose tiles, skids and falls. I hear a hard object, the torch presumably, ricochet off a wall. I'm glad. He doesn't have a nightstick now.

"Ow!" he shrieks.

"Shut up," I hiss.

"What!"

"I said, Shut up. There could be other people in the house." But suddenly I don't think so. If anyone was in the house then they would have come to investigate by now. This gives me a small surge of confidence. This and two other facts: one, that my eyes are already getting accustomed to the dark; and two, that the dark should be to my advantage anyway. After all, I know Chance House and Niker doesn't. Although of course, it will get slightly lighter as we get to the top of the house. The mesh is only on the windows of the first two floors.

"Come on," I say, "get up."

He paws up at me. When our hands meet, he grips mine tightly.

"Shall I go first?" I offer.

"You're joking."

He stumbles past me to where he knows the stairs begin, steadies himself to find the banister. With the banister he can be safe. He thinks. Underfoot is the stripped wallpaper, but he's going carefully. He negotiates it with apparent ease. I let him get a tread or two in front of me. He's gaining confidence, lifting his feet automatically, used now to the depth of tread, the glue-stiff paper. Then, all of a sudden, he's on it.

Sinking in.

"Oh God, oh no! Norbert!"

"It's only lagging," I say, casually.

"What!"

"You know, that spongy stuff they put round boilers, to keep the heat in?" It's under my feet now. The suck and squish of it. Niker is breathing hard and I don't need a 100-watt lightbulb to tell what his

"Yes," I say.

There's a pause into which he could insert the word "sorry," but he doesn't.

"Come on," he says.

We walk side by side up the last of the stairs. The door to Top-Floor Flat, Chance House, is open, just as before. As I expected, there is slightly more light here, partly because of the unmeshed windows but also because two of the rooms look over the front of the house, so there is some filtering streetlight. Niker scans the kitchen, the sitting room, the sledgehammered bathroom, and then sees the front room with the mattress.

"Five-star," he says. "That'll be my room."

"Suit yourself," I say. The back room is pulling me. Somehow, in my imagination, I haven't got further than this: the dark, the fear. Niker. But now there's something else. I think it's David Sorrel. Wanting me in that room, as though there is something to find after all. As though Edith Sorrel's wisdom is in there and, last time, I just missed it.

I turn toward the room. The door is as I left it. Ajar. I begin walking, my body heavy, somnambulant, as though I'm sleepwalking. I don't want Niker to come with me. But he does, following so close behind me he's almost treading on my heels. We pass through the door.

"Ducks," I say. A million duck eyes stare at us.

"I expect Mrs. Sorrel told you," says Niker. "You were discussing home furnishings, then and now, and she told you."

I don't bother to answer that, because I'm moving toward the window with the star of glass cut from it. I feel quite determined, quite peaceful. I am, after all, the sort of boy who can fly.

"What are you doing?" says Niker suddenly.

"Just want to look out the window."

"No," he says.

"Yes."

"No!" He dodges in front of me.

"Get out of my way, Niker."

"What's wrong with you?"

"Nothing's wrong with me."

"The window's broken. You're three floors up."

"I know that, Niker."

"What are you going to do?"

"I told you. I'm going to look out the window."

"That's all?"

"Yes. That's all."

He moves aside, but not so far that he couldn't grab me if he wanted to.

There is light coming through the window. The clouds have cleared. There are stars again. Hundreds of millions of stars. And also a moon. A huge silver disk hung in the sky like some giant coin. It's so beautiful, so perfect, that I want to reach through the hole in the glass and touch it. And I will. But not yet. Not with Niker here.

I turn around, take off my backpack and make a show of searching for a clean space at the back of the room on which to lay my sleeping bag. "Hey—looks like you've got the best deal with that mattress," I say. He watches me arrange things, take out the packet of plain crisps, the bottle of water.

"I think it would be better if we stuck together," he says.

"Thanks," I say. "But no thanks. If you want crisps—"

"No."

"See you in the morning then," I say cheerily.

"I'm not letting you sleep in here by yourself."

"You mean you don't want to sleep in there by yourself."

"No, I don't mean that."

"What do you mean then?"

"I just don't think you should sleep in here."

"Why? Because of David Sorrel?"

"Maybe."

"What are you afraid of, Niker?"

"Me? I'm not afraid of anything."

"Well, push off then." I begin to remove my jacket. "Nighty-night, Niker. Oh—and shut the door, will you?"

Grudgingly, he retreats. "I'll be listening," he says. "If you go anywhere near that window . . ."

"Yes. Yes."

He doesn't shut the door, but the configuration of the rooms is such that I know, even with both doors wide open, that he will not be able to see the star hole window.

I have plenty of time so I wait. Take a sip of water and open one of the bags of crisps. They are crushed, as expected, and I crush them some more, so Niker will think I'm eating. I even wait after I hear the zip of his sleeping bag. Then, just as I think he may be drifting off, he suddenly shouts across the landing: "Did you bring a good book?"

"No, I got the telly," I call back.

"This mattress is disgusting. It's got bird muck on it."

"Well, don't go on. Everyone will want it."

"Fancy a chat? You know, person to person? This long-distance stuff can get expensive."

"No, thanks." I yawn. "I'm on the way out. Just going to tidy up my three-course dinner, then it's bed-byes for me. Curtains."

"Curtains?"

"That's what I said."

"Norbert?"

"Yeah?"

He leaves the sort of pause that my mum leaves before she says "I love you."

Niker says: "There's a piece of piping in my sleeping bag."

"Rusty piping?"

"Yes. How did you know?"

"I've got the same. I think it must be a free sample."

"Norbert?"

"Yes?"

"Why aren't you funny at school?"

"Why aren't you nice at school?"

"Sure you don't need me to join you in the master bedroom?"

"Sure. Night, Niker."

He shuts up after that. I think about waiting until I can hear him snore. But if he doesn't snore that could be a long time. So I give it about five minutes and then I pick a stealthy way across the bare floorboards. Of course one of them creaks, but Niker either doesn't hear or doesn't react. Perhaps he's getting used to the noises the house makes. Perhaps he really is asleep. Please let him be asleep.

And please let there be no clouds. I need the sky to be clear. I need . . . Yes! I arrive at the window and there it is again. My perfect, magnetic moon. You can see why tides follow the moon. I feel the pull myself, the power of that huge planet hanging there, just beyond the broken glass. The latch of the window is old-fashioned, an arm of metal, heavy, pierced like a belt and painted cream. I lift it and know at once that the window is quite free. It will open with the gentlest of pushes.

I push.

And that's when the heavens come into the room, or I go out of it. The moon, the stars, the night wind, the vault of the sky. I inhabit it all and it inhabits me. The freedom, the vastness, the power. And also the beauty. And of course I'm not going to jump. I know that I cannot fly. Not with wings anyway. But I can fly, yes. Can stand bold at the top of Chance House because I have walked up each step of my fear and arrived here. Twice. And that gives the power. Power over myself and power over Niker. Who is still afraid. I breathe deep, inhaling and exhaling the possibilities of this night and, just for a moment, I feel gigantic. I feel capable of anything.

"No!" Niker screams from the door. "Don't do it!" He sprints across the room and rugby-tackles me to the ground.

"Oh no, no—I don't believe it!" His hands are on the back of my sweatshirt. "What have you done! What is this!" he yells.

"Tomato ketchup," I say, or rather I mumble as my face is squashed to the floor.

"It's blood," he says. "It's the shape of a star!"

"Trust me," I say, spitting. "It's tomato ketchup. Courtesy of one Mr. Deep-Fat, Vinney's Chip Shop. I'll tell you about it some other time. Now, do you think I could get up, please?"

He lets me go and then jumps up himself, pulls shut the window and stands guard, blocking the sky.

"What do you think you were doing?" he demands.

I can't tell him I was feeling gigantic, so I just say: "None of your business."

"If you fall out," he says, "they'll blame me. They'll think I pushed you."

"Oh," I say, "is that what's bothering you? Mind you, who'd know? From my position on the concrete, I wouldn't be doing a lot of talking."

"This is not a joking matter."

"Isn't it? I thought everything was a joke with you. Shane Perkiss, Jon Pinkman . . ."

"What have they got to do with anything?"

"They have to do with—grapes." And, for the first time, when I say the word "grapes," I do not feel sick.

"I don't trust you," says Niker.

"You don't trust me!" Very slowly I get up and cross to where my backpack is. I get out an apple. I also get out a penknife.

"Either you sleep in my room," he says, "or I sleep here."

I cut the apple in half. "I'm not shifting."

"Right then, I'll get my gear. And you don't move. You stay right where you are." He's out of the room for less than a minute, but I still have time to prepare eight perfect crescents of apple.

He lays his sleeping bag so close to mine they are almost touching. He must be lonely as well as frightened.

"Apple?"

"No, thanks."

"Oh—go on."

He takes a piece. Looks at me. Bites. "Yeuch."

"It doesn't taste good?"

"It's revolting."

"Oh—perhaps that was the bit I wiped my bum with."

He gags and spits.

Now, I know it's not a very pleasant thing to say and it also isn't true. But I say it because of the Grape Incident. This is what happened. Niker took me and Pinky and Perky into the Dog Leg. They were both new boys, Jon Pinkman and Shane Perkiss, and they wanted to belong, and that meant being on Niker's team. So they did what he asked. And I did it too. Although for me the reason was fear.

"It's only a game," he said. "A dare. This is how you play. . . ."

Each of us was given a grape, a fat green grape. He told us to put it between the cheeks of our bum. And we did. Then there was to be a crawling race. From the first bend in the Dog Leg to the second. Niker had a whistle. He blew it. The person who came last in the race had to eat the grapes. I came last.

Pinky said then, "Surely it's a joke?"

And Niker said, "No." It was a test, an initiation. We'd agreed to take part so we had to abide by the rules. He pushed those grapes into my mouth himself.

"Water?" I offer him now. He didn't offer me any water in the Dog Leg.

He takes the water and swills out his mouth.

"Do you want me to say sorry?" he asks.

"What for?"

"Sorry," he says, and then he says, "Robert."

And of course I should be glad. Because I have dreamed of this moment, rehearsed it a thousand impossible times in my mind: Jonathan Niker apologizing. Jonathan Niker saying sorry to me. But my victory is hollow, sad even. There's something obscene about Niker with his sleeping bag so pathetically close to mine and his head bowed. He looks crushed. Small.

"Forget it," I say. And then after a moment, "No, don't forget it. Because I won't. I'll never forget what you did, Niker." He still looks small. "But don't worry about the apple. It was just one of a really weird bunch Mum got cheap at the market. Want a crisp?"

"No, thanks."

He gets into his sleeping bag and turns away from me. I imagine it will be a long time before he sleeps. But it isn't. Almost immediately he falls into a profound slumber. When the rhythms of his body turn him toward me once again, he looks like a baby. Curled up and peaceful and utterly innocent.

I'm tired now myself. At least my body is tired, exhausted even. But my brain will not let me rest. There is still the matter of David Sorrel. It was David who brought me here, who allowed me, for probably the first time in my life, to feel powerful. And David who I need to repay. I need to know what really happened to him and I need to give something back to Mrs. Sorrel, for she has kept her part of the bargain. She said there was wisdom in this room and there is. But there is obviously something else. Something that she still seeks and I must find. But what? What am I supposed to return to her? I get up and begin to pace. The floor creaks but it neither worries me nor wakes Niker. In fact, after a while, I find it comforting, something predictable, something known.

I don't know how many circuits of the room I make. Maybe fifteen. Maybe twenty. I look in and between things. I push my nails into the dirt cracks of floorboards. I peel off pieces of wallpaper to reveal nothing but dusty plaster. The ducks observe me, unimpressed. There is nothing here. Nothing physical anyhow. Except a couple of feathers. Three feathers, to be precise: small, grayish, unremarkable. Pigeon feathers probably, dropped by some bird that came through the hole in the glass to shelter here a night. Perhaps the same bird, or birds, who shat on Niker's mattress. Not objects likely to radically alter a person's life. But I slip them into my pocket anyway. Then I return to my pacing. When I can walk no more I climb into my sleeping bag. I toss, I turn. I listen to the measured sound of Niker's breathing. Typical. I cannot imagine how, with his bruised body, he is sleeping on this hard, hard floor. But he is sleeping and I am awake. It's because I can't stop thinking and this is what it all comes down to: I wanted the Top-Floor Flat, Chance House, to be the end of things, but now I have to accept that it's only the beginning.

PART TWO

The Coat of

Feathers

11

I'd like to tell you that after spending the night in Chance House, I was never frightened of anything—or anyone—again. Especially not Niker. But that wouldn't be true. I think fear can become a habit. And I'd been afraid of Niker for so long, it had become as natural to me as breathing.

So when, the following morning, Niker and I stand on the concrete outside the kitchen of Chance House and he says, with his face very close to mine: "What happened in there was private. Just between the two of us. Understand?" I do understand. It isn't a threat of the old sort–the one where the tile shard would have been in my throat. But it is, nevertheless, a threat, a statement about the fragility of our new relationship. The tile shard will remain in his pocket, but only if I play the game by his rules.

The first test of the new status quo comes at school on Monday morning.

"Well," says Kate, "are there ducks or aren't there ducks?"

Niker says: "There are ducks."

And I add, without so much as a blink: "Mrs. Sorrel mentioned the duck paper, when we were talking about home furnishings. The sort of things that were fashionable in her day compared with what we have now." Then I smile a goofy smile.

Kate raises an eyebrow. She swings suspicious eyes from Niker's face to mine.

Niker grins. Not a goofy grin. A huge, triumphant grin.

"Norbert!" Kate exclaims, exasperated.

And OK–it makes me miserable. But not that miserable. You see, deep down, I'm not sure that this is Norbert lying on the floor and allowing himself to be tramped on all over again. It occurs to me that maybe this is Robert speaking. Robert saying what he's saying to protect the weaker party. And that weaker party is Niker.

Wesley overhears the conversation.

"You stayed in dat spooky, spooky place?" he says, incredulous.

"Got it in one, Weasel," says Niker.

"And you didn't go no stir-crazy scaredy-cat?"

"No," Niker says, "I did not go no stir-crazy scaredy-cat. Generally speaking, I'm not the scaredy-cat type. Am I, Norbert?"

"No," I say.

Letting him get away with this is less forgivable. Because he was scared that night. Scared of the dark, scared of sleeping by himself, just plain scared. But if I challenge him, who would believe me? Certainly not Wesley. After a while, I barely believe myself. No matter how many times I go over it in my mind, I can't identify the one moment where I can point the finger and say: "It was then, there, that's when Niker freaked, lost it completely." Because you see, when the batteries died, he could just have been angry with me, just as he could have been genuinely concerned about me sleeping alone. But if things shift in my mind, they don't in Niker's. He was right about the ducks. He was not scared. If you say things loud enough and long enough they take on a life of their own. Or that's what I find, listening to Niker, hero of Chance House.

But none of this matters when it comes to Wednesday. On Wednesday we return to the Mayfield Rest Home. All the Elders are gathered in the lounge.

All, that is, except Edith Sorrel. Catherine begins by saying how delighted she is with the work that everyone is making. I, who have made no work, hide behind a plastic palm tree. Catherine smiles, she expects to begin assembling some of the pieces onto the triptych boards next week. In the meanwhile she wants to tell a story. A story told to the Prince, to try to make him throw off his curse of silence.

"There was once a man . . . ," she begins.

It is time for me to slip out. I turn as if I am heading for the toilet and then double back on myself and make for Mrs. Sorrel's room. I feel a strange elation. At last I have something to report. And even if I'm not bearing the treasure Mrs. Sorrel might have hoped for, I have fulfilled my promise. I have been to the Top-Floor Flat, Chance House.

As I put my hand on her door handle I hear the pad of feet behind me. Matron's hand closes over mine.

"You can't go in there," she says.

"I'm Robert," I say, "I'm on the project."

"Even so," says Matron.

"But Mrs. Sorrel's my Elder. I'm making work with her. We're working together."

"Not today you're not," says Matron. "I'm sorry."

This seems, for Matron, to be the end of the discussion. She smiles. I think quickly: choice one, slink away and creep back when she's not looking; choice two, face it out right now.

"Why?" I say, drawing myself up to my full height, which is somewhere near her shoulder. "Why can't I go in?"

Matron tsks. "Mrs. Sorrel is resting."

"She was resting last week. I was very quiet. I didn't wake her. But when she woke up herself, she was glad I was there. She likes me being there."

"This week's different," says Matron. "Mrs. Sorrel is ill."

I haven't taken my hand from the door handle. I tighten my grip. The twist is involuntary, just my wrist twitching, but she hears the click of the catch.

"Come with me this minute," she says, and she almost pushes me down the corridor into her office. She shuts the door.

"Now, young man," she says. "You are going to be off this project if you don't respect the rights of my patients. I repeat, Mrs. Sorrel is ill. She needs to rest. She cannot make any work. I'm sorry."

"She was ill last week," I counter. "Her husband told me she's been ill for ages."

"Not this ill," says Matron emphatically.

"What ill?" I ask.

Matron pauses. When a person is talking about illness and they don't look you in the eye, my mum says it's always cancer. "Is it cancer?" I ask.

"You're a very bold boy," says Matron.

"It's important," I say.

"To whom?"

"To me." And when I say it I realize it's true. Edith Sorrel is not some batty old woman in an old people's home. Edith Sorrel is part of my life. "Is she going to die?" I ask.

Matron looks at me. "Yes," she says. And then she smiles. "But we're all going to die someday, aren't we, Robert?"

"Thanks. Can I go now?"

"Yes, but not to Mrs. Sorrel's room."

"Understood," I say. I go out, close the door and go straight to Mrs. Sorrel's room. One silent twist and I'm in.

They have moved Mrs. Sorrel's bed into the middle of the room. Later Ernest tells me it's so the staff can lift her more easily, turn her. She looks marooned in the bed, pale and drawn and in the wrong place. As though she were some tiny bird who should be out flying round a summer garden but got caught short by winter.

"Mrs. Sorrel," I call softly. "It's me. Robert."

"Robert," she says, but her eyes don't open. "Robert."

"Matron says I can't talk to you. Can I talk to you, Mrs. Sorrel?"

"I don't like Matron," says Edith.

"I don't like her either."

"Well, that's that then." Edith Sorrel opens her eyes. She peers. "Lift me up," she commands.

I dither. I feel strong enough to lift her, but I don't dare because she looks so fragile. I fear to break her.

"Come on," she says, "pillows!" She begins struggling. So I put my arm behind her and try to get her into a more upright position. With her own efforts, and a cushion from the chair, we manage some sort of sitting. As she moves, pain passes over her face, but she says nothing.

"Come nearer."

I obey.

She scrutinizes my face. "You're different," she says.

"No, no, it's just me. Robert."

"You've got bigger."

"Maybe you've got smaller," I joke.

"No," she says. "Not your height. You're bigger inside. You've been, haven't you? I can see it in your eyes. You've been there. Top-Floor Flat, Chance House. You've done it!"

"Yes."

"You're such an amazing boy. You're a brave, brave boy. I knew you could do it. I knew it."

"But there's nothing there," I say quickly. "I looked and looked. I spent the night there. But there's nothing. Nothing at all. Unless you count a broken window, some duck wallpaper and a bunch of feathers."

"Feathers?" she says.

"Only pigeon feathers. Nothing special."

"Show me."

I take the three feathers from my trouser pocket. As well as being gray and scrubby, they are now squashed. She takes them in her bony fingers, begins a rhythmic smoothing of the flights.

"Once," she begins out of nowhere, "there was a man who dreamed of Firebirds. One midsummer day, as he rested from his labors in the forest, a beautiful creature came down from the sky. It was hot and, needing to bathe, she slipped off her coat of golden feathers and dived, naked, into the forest pool. The man thought he had never seen a more beautiful woman in all his life. And, as she swam, he took her coat of golden feathers and hid it. When she emerged from the pool she was distraught at the loss. But the man said, 'Come with me. I will give you shelter.'

"Knowing she could not fly away, the woman went with him. He was a good man. Gentle. In time they had a child together. A son, whom the woman loved with all her Firebird heart. When the child was about twelve, he called to his mother; 'Mother, mother, come quickly. Look what I have found while playing in the forest.' And she followed the sound of her beloved's voice and discovered him holding the coat of golden feathers."

She tells this story not as Catherine would have done, with eyes open and alert, but as if she's in a trance, telling the story from inside out, as if it were something she knows only because she's lived inside it all of her life.

"Get me my pink sweater," she commands then.

"What?"

"My pink sweater," she repeats irritably. "Second drawer down."

And I remember how she called for her pink dressing gown after she told me how Ernest had stopped her singing, and how angry she seemed then too.

"Quickly!" she says.

There is only one pink item in the drawer. It's not a pullover sweater, but a short-sleeved cardigan buttoned, with tiny pearls, to the neck. The color is pale, delicate, flesh-toned.

"Bring it here."

I take it to her.

"Make me a coat of feathers," she says.

"What!"

"Make it," she says. "Sew it. Sew the feathers on."

"I can't do that!"

"What do you mean 'can't'?" she says. And, all of a sudden, she doesn't look quite so frail.

"Can't sew," I say, helplessly. "I can't sew!"

"A boy who can go to the top of Chance House can do anything," she says.

"Except sew," I say solidly.

"Get a needle," she says. "Bedside cabinet."

I don't know who's pulling my strings but I go to the bedside cabinet. On the bottom shelf is a small blond straw basket decorated with bright red raffia strawberries. It contains scissors, needles, thread.

"Use white," she says.

"What?"

"White cotton."

Then I say it: "This is mad," I say.

She gives me the witchy, see-right-through-you look. "It's work," she replies. "Our work. We're supposed to be making work, aren't we?"

"Yes . . . but . . ."

"But what?"

"But that work is supposed to be something that makes a connection between the past and the present, between your life and mine. A wisdom."

"Exactly," she says, triumphantly. "Now thread the needle."

"I can't."

"Do it, David!"

"David?"

"Just do it."

"David, you called me David. My name's Robert."

"Is it?"

"You know it is! David is the name of your son. Your dead son."

"Dead? David's dead? Who says David's dead?" She looks utterly stricken. A little bird with an arrow in her heart.

"No," I cry. "I mean—not now. Not recently. Years ago. Thirty years. He died when he was twelve. Yes?"

"No," she says. "Oh no. No, no, no, no. Don't let David be dead. Don't let my baby be dead."

And this is how Matron, coming in bearing a small plastic pot of pills, finds us. Me, sitting mute and horrified on the bed. Edith Sorrel in it, howling like an animal. I look at Matron and Matron looks at me. I have never been more grateful to see anyone in all of my life.

"You!" splutters Matron. "How dare you! Get out of here, you lying little . . ."

Mrs. Sorrel rises. She towers. She stops crying. "Don't you ever speak to him like that," she says. "Do you hear me?"

But I'm not waiting for a second chance. I'm right off that bed, I'm going wherever Matron tells me.

"Sorry," I mumble at Mrs. Sorrel.

Mrs. Sorrel makes a Herculean grab. She has my hand. Her grip is bone to bone.

"Don't go," she says. "Don't leave me. Please."

"What exactly is going on here?" asks Matron.

"Robert is making work," says Mrs. Sorrel. "He's making me a coat of feathers."

"You're supposed to be resting," says Matron.

"I haven't been able to rest for thirty years," says Mrs. Sorrel.

"Then take these," says Matron quickly, and she presents Mrs. Sorrel with the pills in the plastic cup. From the jug by Mrs. Sorrel's bed, she pours a glass of water. "Here."

Mrs. Sorrel lets go of me and beats her bird hand at Matron. Plastic cup and pills go flying. But she has overreached herself and the effort makes her wince.

"The pills are for the pain," Matron observes. "They'll help."

"Nothing helps," says Mrs. Sorrel. "Nothing has ever helped with the pain." She looks at me. "Except Robert. Robert helps. Robert's a brave boy. Robert's a wonderful boy. Robert is going to make me a coat of feathers. Aren't you, Robert?"

"Yes," I announce then. "Of course."

12

Question: Who's the bigger bully? Jonathan Niker or Edith Sorrel? *Go to the top of Chance House.* OK, sure, anything you say. *Make me a coat of feathers.* Great idea, I'll start right now. Perhaps it's not just "victim" I have etched into my forehead, but "daft" as well. Norbert No-Brain-at-All. Norbert Push-Him-Over-He's-a-Piece-of-Cake. Maybe I'm just grumpy because of this needle.

Have you ever tried to thread a needle? Fact: No matter how wide the eye of the needle is, the cotton is always wider. Fact: No matter how carefully you cut the cotton to stop it splaying, it splays. Does that deter you? It does not. You just keep on trying. You line up cotton and needle, steady your hand, push and bonanza! You miss. Again. That's when you check to see whether you have a hand or a bunch of bananas at the end of your arm. No question. It's the bunch of bananas. But as persistence is one of your finer qualities, you try again. This time you see the cotton come out the other side! Hurrah! Hurray! You whoop with joy, with triumph, only to find that the cotton has in fact simply passed behind the needle and (while you've been whooping) dropped onto the floor.

"Need any help there?" Mum has come into the room and is rootling around in the dirty linen basket.

"No, thanks."

"What are you doing?"

What does it look like I'm doing? Reading a comic? "I'm trying to thread this needle."

"Why?"

Because I told a batty old woman I'd make her a coat of pigeon feathers, of course. No reply.

Mum, with a kindly expression: "Suck the cotton."

"What?"

"Suck the end. It makes it easier to thread."

I suck the end of the cotton. Guess what? The cotton stops being splayed. In fact I'd have to describe it as becoming pointed, sharp even. I approach the eye of the needle. One swift forward thrust and there we are, the needle is threaded. It's threaded! I pull the cotton through. I am a genius. Now for the knot. Carefully I make a loop of cotton and push the un-needled end through the hole. Then I pull the thread tight. Easy enough—but there is no knot. How can there be no knot? I run the thread between a disbelieving finger and thumb, and there it is. The knot. You'd need a magnifying glass to see it. I try again. A second knot. Also minuscule. And, irritatingly, nowhere near the first knot. I jerk the cotton (could be anger, could be frustration) and, at the other end of the thread, the needle does a backward flip to land in its preferred position on the floor.

"Bad luck," says Mum. She retrieves needle and thread. "Watch." She licks her index finger, wraps the end of the cotton around it, rubs the join between finger and thumb, slides the rubbed loop free and somehow contrives to pull a knot out of nowhere with the nail of her middle finger. "See?"

"Erm . . ."

Then there's a flash of steel and the needle's threaded again. She hands it to me. "Can I ask what you're trying to do?"

"Sew," I say, rather ungratefully.

"Anything in particular?"

"Feathers."

"Feathers?"

"On a sweater." I indicate the flesh-tone pink cardigan.

"Oh. Are you doing a play?"

A play. This is the wonderful thing about the human brain. It's always trying to make sense of things, even when they don't make sense.

"Not exactly."

"What then?"

"I'm making a coat of feathers. It's part of the project. With the old people."

"Oh, right. I see. A kind of artistic expression of how flying has changed from their day to yours?"

Good old Mum. Brain in overdrive. "Something like that."

Mum looks at the feathers. "Have you only got three?"

"I'm going to get more."

And as soon as I say it I know that I am. Because of course, I'm going to make a real coat of feathers. Just as Mrs. Sorrel asked. No matter how long it takes. The piece is already complete in my mind. A hundred large, dark feathers sewn on first and spaced to allow lighter, smaller feathers to be stitched on top. All the feathers matched and gradated, culminating in some of those tiny, really fluffy pure white feathers, sewn around the neckline, and dotted over the body like down on a bird's breast.

"Well, mind you wash your hands afterward. I'm not quite sure how clean those feathers are," says Mum, returning to her work at the linen basket.

"Mum . . ."

"Yes?"

"How long does it take someone to die of cancer?"

I spent some considerable time last night trying to think of a way to work this question into the conversation so it sounded natural. As you see, I failed.

Mum pauses, dirty socks suspended in midair. "Depends what cancer."

"Liver," I say.

"Who do you know with liver cancer?" asks Mum.

"No one."

I didn't intentionally look at Mrs. Sorrel's medical notes. They were just there, on Matron's desk, thrusting themselves under my nose.

Mum sits down on the edge of the bed. "Real liver cancer," she says, "is very quick but very rare. That's where the primary—or first—tumor is actually in the liver. Most cancer in the liver comes from a secondary tumor, and then the prognosis is rather better."

"Weeks?" I ask. "Months?" A pause. "Years?"

"Not years. No. But whether months or weeks, that really depends at what stage the tumor is diagnosed."

"So you don't really know."

"Well, I am fielding a little in the dark here, yes, Robert."

"What about, about, you know, when you get better for no apparent reason?"

"Spontaneous remission? It happens. Not very common though, I'm afraid." She looks at me. "Are we talking Mrs. Sorrel here?"

"Maybe."

"I'm sorry, Robert."

"Don't be," I say. "She's not dead yet."

"Is there anything I can help with?"

"Yes. Can you show me how to do that knot again?"

She shows me. Then she hangs about while I fumble with the needle, the thread, the cardigan and the feather. She doesn't actually say anything until I've sewn the front of the cardigan to the back of it and the feather has slipped out of its binding and onto the floor.

"Here," she says, and she starts by unbuttoning the cardigan. "It's easier if you're only working with one layer. Put the needle through from the back, so you don't see the knot. . . ."

"No, no, I want that feather at the top, coming down from the shoulder."

"Very well. Put it here then. I doubt if you'll get it

to hold unless you actually sew round the flight. Or maybe you could push the needle through the quill itself?"

"Yes," I say. "Do that. Push it right through." I want the coat to be strong. Safe.

The job is harder than she expects. "You need a thimble."

I provide her with the rubber bottom of a stapler. She pushes and the needle goes through. A couple of cotton loops later and the feather is secure.

"Thank you," I say, "thank you very much."

"Next?" She's reaching for a second feather.

"No," I say. "I want to do it."

"Course," she says, deftly securing the needle just below the feather and handing me the cardigan. "Your project, after all. Marvelous if it teaches you to sew. Good old Mrs. Sorrel. That must be a change from her day too."

I don't know if this is meant to be ironic. It sounds ironic. But Mum's not normally the ironic type. So I just keep smiling and nod in the general direction of the dirty socks. She leaves.

The next problem is how to get the thread from the left shoulder to the right—which is where I want to put the second feather. I have this idea that the Chance House feathers should be spaced, two on the front and one on the back. The symmetry of the coat is going to be important as well as the color, the texture. To work as the Firebird coat, it all has to be right.

If I were Mum, I'd simply cut the thread and start again—but that would mean a new knot and I'm none too confident about that. But I can't sew across the opening of the cardigan, because then Mrs. Sorrel will not be able to get it on. And that of course is the point. Mrs. Sorrel is going to wear this coat.

Solution. Sew the back feather on first. Obvious really. I run long and not very elegant stitches under the sleeve to get the needle to the right place. Then I hold the feather firmly and push and push with the stapler back until the needle goes through the quill. As I loop the needle back around I prick myself. Blood beads between my finger and the quill and, as I try to brush it away, I smear it slightly on the cardigan. Of course, with all the feathers I'm going to sew on top, no one will see this tiny mark. But I will know it's there. I take it as a good omen that some of my life's blood has flowed already—willy-nilly—into this coat.

There is not enough thread left to sew the third feather, so I have to fasten off the remaining cotton and cut a new length. This time I'm quicker, both with the threading and the knot. And I'm grateful, not just for my sake but for Mrs. Sorrel's. Time is limited. The question is—how limited? As there seems no answer to that, I'll just have to work as quickly as I can. Every day, every hour, will count. Perhaps every minute. Just as each and every feather will count. The thicker the coat the better, the more likely to succeed.

So where can I get more feathers? The graveyard obviously. With such a colony of pigeons the churchyard must have a constant fall of feathers. I pull the third Chance House feather tight and tie off the cotton. Still an hour of daylight left. I'll go to the graveyard now. What shall I tell my mother? The truth I suppose.

"Just going out, Mum."

"Where?"

"St. Michael and All Angels."

"The church?"

"Yes. The church."

"Why?"

"Get some feathers."

"At this time?"

"It's homework, Mum. I have to."

"It's raining, Robert."

"Fine. I'll wear my raincoat."

"Robert . . ."

I'm out of the house. It is raining. That thin, cold rain that drives liquid icicles down the back of your neck. But it's only a shower. By the time I reach the churchyard, it's stopped. I begin my search, scanning the grass around the older graves. Cigarette packet, bottle top, sodden tissue. A pigeon lands at my feet. Then another. And another. They've been sheltering around the tower of the church and now they are flying, thirty, forty, fifty of them, to my feet.

"Anyone fancy donating a tail feather?"

The pigeons mill, unconcerned.

I resume my search. Empty pill packet, cider bottle, single yellow crocus. The birds move with me, circling with the perfect rhythm of passengers at railway stations, a flow without touch. Perhaps they don't want to get too near. Perhaps they recognize my desperation, my intent. Where are the discarded feathers? Crisp packet. Dog poo. Tombstone of Charity Ann Slaughter.

Feather. Feather! It's gray, drenched, muddy, the barbs of the flight separated with the weight of water. I pick it up. Just as I pick up every feather I find in the next hour. The thin, the straggly, the waterlogged, I fold each as a treasure into my pocket. As I stoop the birds around me coo, a throaty, warbling, love-nest noise.

I started at the outer reaches of the churchyard, but I'm coming in now. Coming closer. Approaching the back of David Sorrel's grave. Of course a pigeon gets there before me. A brown-and-white one that hops up onto David's tombstone and starts to preen.

And suddenly it seems disrespectful so I lift my hand to shoo him away. But he won't go.

"Go on, beat it!" I open my mouth to say. But nothing comes out. Because I've arrived in front of the grave. The white marble chippings are strewn with feathers. But also with blood. A bird has been dismembered there. It's the scene of a kill.

I crouch down. I want to touch. But also I don't. It's that Chance House feeling again—being both drawn and repelled in the same moment. I don't know how long I crouch there, immobile. There are enough feathers to sew both sleeves, or most of the breast of the coat, but some of them are still fleshed together, half a wing lies broken there.

How came the kill to be in this place? What is David trying to tell me? Is it a gift of feathers from him, to say I'm on the right track? Or a warning—a coat of feathers kills? Or is it just me, doing what I accused my mother of, trying to make sense of something that doesn't make any sense? Trying to draw meaning from something that is simply nature, simply coincidence?

"What is it?" I say aloud.

"Urban foxes," says a voice behind me.

I spin around. Ernest Sorrel towers above. His coat is black and flowing.

"Hello, Robert," he says.

"Mr. Sorrel." He's carrying a bunch of narcissi.

"It's getting late," he says. "Should you be out?"

I jump up, brush off my knees. "I'm just on my way home."

"How did you know?" he asks then.

"What?"

"About David? Did she tell you? Did Edith tell you?"

"No."

"So how did you find out?"

"By chance," I say. Which is true and not true. I fell here that day by chance. But I came that day from Chance House. Which was not chance.

"Edith is gravely ill," he says.

"I know. But she's going to get better. I'm going to make her better."

Ernest laughs quietly. "You do make her better," he says.

"No, really," I say. "I'm going to make her a coat of feathers. Firebird feathers. It'll make her well."

"Firebird—the Firebird story? Did she tell you that?"

"Yes."

"It was my fault. I took away her coat of feathers."

"What?"

"I took it away. The thing that made her fly. That's what she said. I stopped her singing. And then, and then . . ." He falters, drops to his knees.

"And then?" I whisper.

But he doesn't answer me, begins to clear the debris from David's grave.

"It'll be all right," I tell him. "I'm going to make the coat. She asked me to. It's what she wants. It'll be all right. It'll come right."

"No," Ernest says. "It's too late." He picks up the stripped ribs, which are all that remain of the pigeon carcass. Puts aside the broken wing. "Years too late."

"I need the feathers," I say.

"What?"

"Those feathers, the ones in your hand. I need them."

"Why?"

"Firebird feathers." I'm sure now. David, Ernest, the feathers. All in the same place at the same time. It can't be chance. David wants me to have these feathers. Mrs. Sorrel wants me to have them. Out of death life. Life. Surely life. "Give them to me, please."

He does as I ask without comment. Then he returns his attention to the grave, taking the dead daffodils from the vase and replacing them with the fresh narcissi.

"Will you be at the Sharing?" I ask.

"What's that?"

"The presentation, a week tomorrow. Friday. The exchange of work between us and the Elders."

He pulls himself stiffly to his feet. There are two damp patches on the front of his coat, where his knees have pressed on the earth.

"If Edith's there," he says, "I'll be there." He looks at me. "If."

And I know what he's trying to tell me. It's the time limit.

13

I don't just clean my hands, I clean the feathers. I wash each of them with soap; I rub the quill, the vane, gently easing apart the barbs of the flight and then smoothing them together again. I want each barb to lie as neatly and as perfectly as on the day it was made. I dispose of mud, of crushed bone and other sticky stuff I don't want to inquire too closely into. Then I begin the drying. First with paper towels, just gentle pats, and then with Mum's hair dryer. At first I turn it on full, but that blasts the barbs apart again, so I learn to keep it on low, blowing lightly from a distance, making the air follow the direction of the barbs. With patience I even manage to coax some fluffiness back into the downy part of each feather, the place where flight meets quill.

The hum of the hair dryer brings Mum.

"Robert . . ."

"Yes?"

"What *are* you doing?"

"Blow-drying feathers." Doesn't she have a hospital to go to?

"For goodness' sake."

"Well, you did say you didn't know how clean feathers were, so I'm cleaning them."

She picks one up, smells it. "You never used my rose geranium soap!"

"Sorry, Mum."

"Really, Robert."

I've a feeling things are going to get worse and they do. When the feathers are clean and dry I begin sewing again. Up till supper, after supper and then when I'm supposed to be sleeping. She spots my light. Comes in.

"You'll ruin your eyes," she says. "Sewing when you're tired is a very bad idea."

"I'm not tired."

"Don't be cheeky," she says, switching off the lamp.

But it's not cheek. I'm really not tired. If I need to stay awake for the next week, then that's what I'll do. If I need to sew by torchlight, then I'll do that too. I'm on a mission. I got to the top of Chance House and I'll get to the end of this coat. *A boy who's been to the top of Chance House can do anything.* Mrs. Sorrel made me fly and I shall make her fly. Whatever Mum says, whatever . . .

"Robert, switch out that light. Now!"

I switch it out.

But not before I've set my alarm for five-thirty. As it happens I wake before the alarm anyway. While night changes into day, I sew. It's a strange sensation being awake when everyone else is asleep. It's strange sewing in the silence and the half-dark. I feel like one of those mythical women at their looms, the Lady of Shalott, or Odysseus' wife, Penelope, weaving to ward off the suitors while her husband is still away, sewing by day and unpicking at night. Only I sew by day and sew by night. Day and night. But it is still not going fast enough and there are not enough feathers. I have to have more feathers.

I have a quick breakfast and leave early for school. I don't have to explain myself because Mum's on earlies too, and she's out of the house before me. Of course I go via the graveyard, I can't help myself, even though I picked the place clean yesterday. I expect nothing.

So it's a gift to see one pure white, perfectly clean and dry feather on the tomb of Charity Ann Slaughter. A breast feather definitely. Gratefully, I stow it in my inside jacket pocket. Then I make for the beach.

I've argued with myself about whether I'm allowed to mix pigeon and seagull feathers and decided that I am. My Firebird coat was never meant to be red or orange. It was meant to be gray and white, this is what Mrs. Sorrel chose when she chose the Chance House feathers. So I'm just following her lead. I know she would approve. What matters is the coat, getting it finished in time, and there will never be enough pigeon feathers.

The wind carries the tang of seaweed to me a street before I reach the beach. When it's very windy the seagulls come inland. Today they are wheeling above the water's edge. Wheeling and screaming. I cross the promenade and come down the steps near the breakwater.

A feather. Immediately a feather, an omen. Caught in the stones by the bottom step. Again white. Again perfect. As if it had just that moment descended from heaven. I pick it up. Three droplets of water sit proud on the flight, like dew on an early-morning flower. I don't think I've ever seen a more beautiful feather. Thank you, God. Thank you, seagull. I unzip my jacket pocket and slip it inside.

I spend an hour on the beach, until my fingers are wind-frozen. I find proud tail feathers and little puffs of fluff, so light you'd think the wind would have carried them away. But it has not, and there they are, waiting for me. I gather them all. Even the two feathers I find stuck together with tar.

I arrive at school as the bell goes for assembly. I dutifully follow the other children into the hall. But what I want to do is sew, to begin immediately. I have the cardigan lodged inside my schoolbag, neatly folded inside its own protective Sainsbury's bag. My fingers itch with the wanting. But I have to be careful. The project is private. Something just between me and Mrs. Sorrel. What I mean is I don't want Niker to get wind of it. I don't even want Kate to know. Where Niker might scoff, she would ask questions.

"Why are you doing it? What's it for?"

If Kate asked that, I'd have to tell her. I'd have to say, "I'm making this coat because I believe it will save Mrs. Sorrel's life."

Yes, now I've said it. What I've barely been admitting to myself. I think a coat of pigeon feathers will save an old woman's life. Even Catherine, the storyteller, wouldn't believe a story like that. But I believe it. I believe it with all my heart.

So that's why I lock myself in the toilet at break time. Take out the coat and sew. There's not a lot of light and the cistern is one of those old-fashioned ones with a chain. The rubber end keeps banging into my cheek. But at least it's private.

Least it is until Niker spots my feet.

"What you doing in there?" he asks.

No answer.

"Delivering a baby?"

No answer. Surely other people have shoes like mine?

"Or have you got the runs?"

"I think he's going for the *Guinness Book of Records*," says Weasel's voice. "Longest dump in history. Get your gas masks, boys."

Niker laughs. Then I hear the door to the corridor open and close and I think they've gone. When the bell goes I come out, and there they are standing directly opposite me, arms folded.

Niker eyes my bag. "What's the game, Norbie?"

"No game."

"What's in the bag?"

"Nothing."

"Well, let's see this nothing, then." He makes toward the bag. Weasel follows.

"Touch that bag and you're dead."

Wesley hesitates, but more from surprise than fear, I think. Niker keeps on coming.

"Chance House," I say then. Niker stops midstep.

"Come any closer and I'll tell Wesley about Chance House."

Wesley turns to look at Niker. Niker's mouth twists furiously. "Talking of dead," he says, "you just wait!" Then he's gone. Wesley gives me a quizzical look and then trots after his leader.

For the rest of the day I make sure I am never alone and I never, once, take my hand from the strap of my bag. When the final bell goes, I'm out of that school faster than you would be if all the Furies in hell were after you. I don't even stop when Miss Raynham's voice cuts through the air: "Robert Nobel, come back here at once and *walk* across the playground or else . . ."

I don't hear the else, I'm halfway down the street by then. I don't stop running till I get home. Mum lets me in and says my tea's on the table. But I want to sew so I let it go cold.

"Remind me," says Mum, "not to bother to cook for you. If you want cold, you can look in the fridge."

I don't answer, I'm concentrating on a very difficult piece of oversewing, placing the pure white feather exactly between two dark gray ones.

"You're becoming like your father," says Mum.

I don't answer that either. She opens her mouth to speak again but the phone interrupts her.

"Hello," she says irritably. "Oh, speak of the devil.

Hello, Nigel." She listens a moment and then she holds out the phone to me. "Dad for you," she says.

"Tell him I'll call him back."

"What!" shrieks my mother.

While she's shrieking I have plenty of time to contemplate my error. It's clearly a big one—saying I'd call him later. So why did I do it? One, because I am at a very delicate stage of sewing; two, because I didn't want Mum to think I had time to talk to Dad but not time to eat her dinner; three, because Dad hasn't bothered to call since he let me down that Saturday so I don't see why I should do him any favors; and finally, and most importantly, I am fully and completely engaged in the rather more important job of saving someone's life.

"Robert," shrieks my mother, "you have become obsessed! Put that sewing down! Now!"

"Sewing?" I hear the disembodied voice of my father say. "Sewing!"

I finish my loop and put down the sewing. I take the phone Mum's handing me for fear she will have an epileptic seizure.

"Yes?"

"Hello, Robert."

"Hello, Dad." Another one of our startlingly intimate conversation begins.

"Whatcha been doing?"

"Things."

"What's this about sewing?"

"Nothing."

He sighs. "How about a week today? Friday?"

"What for?"

"A visit, Robert. Me coming to see you."

"Sorry, Dad, no can do."

That's when Mum starts pinching my elbow and mouthing wildly.

"No," I repeat, mainly for her benefit. "I'm sorry. It's the Sharing."

"The what?" says Dad.

"It's a project I'm involved in. With some old people. Everyone who's been involved has to go. It's a school thing, I can't get out of it."

"I'm not talking school time," says Dad. "I couldn't be with you before seven anyhow."

"That's when it is," I say solidly. "Seven o'clock."

"They won't miss you," hisses Mum. "Make an exception, Robert, please."

"No, sorry," I say into the phone. "Bye." I hand the phone to my mother, whose mouth is hanging open as though she's trying to catch flies. Then I collect my sewing and adjourn upstairs.

As I go up I hear snatches of the conversation. It's about my sewing, about my obsession, about how I'm going completely bonkers and it's all Dad's fault. At least this seems to be the shrieked implication. If he paid me some more attention then I wouldn't be turning out this way. How is she supposed to cope on her own, and hold down a job to make enough money for both of us to live, and keep me from going bonkers at the same time?

Of course, I can't hear what Dad is replying but I expect it's along the lines of, It's a trifle difficult to visit the little obsessive, if he won't be visited. And in any case it's not true about the money because he sends her some and what's more doesn't she realize he has responsibilities to a new family now? Yes, she jolly well does realize that! Bang, the phone goes down.

Then I hear her crying and of course I can't bear that so I go downstairs and say sorry. Then I eat my cold supper and say how nice it is. But I have to tell you, stone-cold spaghetti bolognaise is not nice. Then I say I have some homework to do and I go back upstairs. Later she comes up and sits on my bed. I'm no fool, so when I hear her coming, I shove the cardigan under the duvet and get out my book. She obviously isn't concentrating much better than I am, because when I look down, I find I'm holding the book upside down.

"They've just rung to ask if I can work the seven P.M. shift," she says. "Will you be all right?"

"Of course." Question is, will she be all right? An

early shift. A late shift. And she can't have had more than five hours' sleep last night. No wonder she's exhausted.

"I'm sorry to shout," she says.

"It's OK."

"You know I love you?"

"Yes."

"And Dad does too."

I don't reply.

"He does."

"Yes," I say.

She ruffles my hair, like she used to when I was a baby. "Promise me to turn your light off on time?"

"Promise."

"OK, bye, sweetheart."

"Bye, Mum."

Downstairs I hear the kettle whistling. She must be making a thermos of coffee. She only does that when she thinks they're going to be really busy. A few minutes later there's the bang of the front door.

This gives me an opportunity and, if I'm to honor my promise and turn my lights off on time, I have to go now. I have sewn both sleeves of the cardigan and completed the left breast. The right one still needs more of the white downy feathers, and the back of the coat is still distinctly patchy. But it is coming on and Mrs. Sorrel needs to know that.

I finish off the feather I was sewing before Mum came in and secure the thread. Then I fold the coat carefully, lengthways, following the line of the feathers themselves. It can't be folded breadthways now. It's beginning to take on a life of its own. It's no longer a pink cardigan, in fact you can barely see pink at all. What you can see is bird, fledgling bird.

I pack the coat in its plastic bag and slip out into the dusk. From school we go by bus to the Mayfield Rest Home, but it's not a long walk. Especially if you know the shortcuts. Which I do. It's a beautiful evening, clear and already starlit. Not unlike the night I went to Chance House with Niker. I thread my way through the streets. The only danger at the home is Matron. But I'm not afraid of her. Mayfield is not a prison. People are allowed to visit. Especially when they're welcomed, wanted. The walk takes about half an hour. The flesh of my face is chill but inside I'm glowing. I feel alive, happy.

The Mayfield door has a bell for new visitors and a security code lock for patients' friends and relatives. I paid careful attention last time Catherine pressed the buttons. 1,9,1,7. Nineteen seventeen. Possibly the birth year of one of the residents. I press the numbers and the door buzzes. I'm quickly in. From here I have to pass through the dining room to get to Mrs. Sorrel's room, but it's past the residents' eating time and in any case Matron is never involved in kitchen duties. So it's just a matter of slipping quietly through. Which I do. Then it's only half a corridor. I've already decided not to knock on Mrs. Sorrel's door. I don't want to draw unnecessary attention to myself. So I just walk casually down the hall and let myself into her room.

She's asleep, of course. Breathing lightly, little flutters of air coming from her mouth. But she doesn't look natural. She looks like a Snow White in a glass case, her body lying like someone else has arranged it and then brushed her hair while she was asleep, so that it lies too straight on the pillow.

"Mrs. Sorrel."

She does not respond.

"Mrs. Sorrel," I say more loudly, "it's Robert."

"Mmm?" she says from a long way out.

"Robert. Robert Nobel."

"Mmm." Her voice sinks away again.

"I've done the coat. Well, started it. It's here. I've brought it."

"Ah?"

I unwrap the fledgling thing. Lift it to her hand, which lies so still on the bed. I run one of the soft white feathers against her finger. Her hand twitches and she reaches, scrabbles for it. A hold, then a relax, a stroke.

"You are such a good boy," she says, and her eyes open.

I lift the coat up, show her glazed eyes the downy breast, the gray-white sleeves, the strong, thick undercoat.

"It's beautiful," she says.

"It's not finished," I say quickly.

"Beautiful," she repeats. "Let me . . ."

I bring the coat close to her hand again and let her hold it, stroke it. I watch her maneuver herself upward, so as to see and feel it better. Is it just my imagination that thinks she moves more easily for the touch of it? She turns it over, feels the weight of it. Now she is almost upright, and I haven't helped her at all. Nor have her eyes expressed pain.

"When will it be finished?"

"Soon," I say. "Soon as possible. I work on it day and night."

"God bless you, Robert Nobel." She smiles. The whole of her pale face lit by that smile, as if someone has put a match to a candle deep inside her. I wish Ernest were here to see this face of hers.

"Is it dark?" she asks then.

"Sorry?"

"Outside," she says, "is it dark, is it night?"

"Yes."

"And is it clear? Are there stars?"

"Yes. There are stars."

"Then take me out," she says.

When I don't reply immediately—because I cannot see how I can possibly take her out—she adds one word: "Please."

And then I know I will move heaven and earth to take her into the starlight.

"There's a chair," she says simply. A wheelchair by the side of her bed, which I haven't noticed until this moment. She pushes aside her bedcovers. She's wearing a thin white cotton nightdress.

"It's cold," I say, in a tone that makes me sound a little like my mother.

"There are rugs," she says.

The bed is higher than the chair and I don't see how I can get her from one to the other. But, of her own accord, she swings her legs over the edge of the bed. Maybe they have given her more of those drugs for pain. Maybe it's the coat, which she still has clutched in her hands.

"Bring it closer."

I locate the brake of the chair and wheel it alongside the bed.

"Put your hands round my waist."

I do as she asks. She can't weigh more than a sparrow. I lift her into the chair.

"Now the rugs."

As I get them from the cupboard I think this is the first time I have ever been with her and she hasn't been angry. Her calmness, her gentleness are strange– but also sweet.

I wrap four rugs about her, over her knees, around her shoulders, I cocoon her in warmth. Under the rugs, clasped on her lap, lies the unfinished coat.

"Now," she says. "Are we ready?"

We are. I wedge the door open so I can get the chair out.

"Left," she commands. "Go left!" Do I detect an urgency now? Or is it just that, like me, she's alert to the danger of encountering Matron? As I push her quickly down the corridor, I feel like an escapee.

"Use the fire door. It isn't alarmed. Just push it. Now."

I brake, push the double iron bar and the door swings wide. The cold assaults us but I see her nostrils flare and she breathes hard in, as though it's years since she last inhaled the night.

"Through," she says. "Now!"

I wheel her out. Behind us the door closes sound-lessly. It is just the back of the home, flat concrete paths, a spill of light from nearby windows, some straggly plants in bare earth beds, a wooden bench. But it is immediately clear that these earthly things do not hold Edith Sorrel's attention. She leans backward,

her neck lengthening, her chin up, because she's looking up, up and beyond. Edith Sorrel's body is not
bound by this chair, this earth. She's not of these
paths, she's reaching up, traveling up toward those
bright and far-off stars.

"Edith," I cry.

"Yes?" she says, and turns a radiant face to mine.
Then she adds, "Won't be long now." Her eyes are
dark and sparkling, as though some part of that sky
and those stars has entered her head. And I want to
pull her back, from whatever brink she's on. Just as
Niker wanted to pull me back from the window in
Chance House. But Edith doesn't want to be pulled,
just as I didn't. Edith is happy, just as I was. Just as we
both are. Inhabiting our nights.

"I love you, Robert Nobel," she says.

And I don't say "I love you" back, because that
would be mad. But somebody says it. "I love you too."

And afterward I don't know whether it was me or
Ernest. But I don't think it was him because he comes
pouring through the door and this is what he says:

"Oh my God, Edith. Edith! I went to the room.
You weren't there. You were gone. I thought . . . I
thought . . ."

Edith looks at him cascading there and she says,
lifting her hand to me: "He's come back."

And Ernest says: "Yes."

Then Edith looks at her husband, concentrates. "And you've come back," she says, with an air of mild astonishment.

"I never left," he answers.

And I think then he might lean and kiss her and that maybe she will accept that kiss, but it doesn't happen because Matron bulls through the doorway.

"Are you insane!" she says.

"Not anymore," says Edith Sorrel.

And that shuts Matron up, not least because, as Ernest tells me later, it is apparently four days since anyone in the home has heard Edith speak a word.

But Matron still needs to do some spluttering and I am the obvious target.

"You!" she splutters. "It's you again!"

"Take me in, Robert," says Mrs. Sorrel. And I do. Ernest flows quietly behind us.

"She could catch her death out there," continues Matron, shutting the fire door.

"I don't think so." That's Ernest, supporting me.

We wheel her back to her room.

"We can manage, thank you," says Ernest to Matron. Matrons huffs but that is all she can do. She is not needed and not wanted. She leaves.

Together Ernest and I remove the rugs and lift Edith back onto the bed. She is still holding the coat of feathers. Her eyes are shut. She looks exhausted but peaceful.

"I have to go now," I say. "I promised my mum."

"You were right," says Ernest. "You do make her better."

"It's the coat," I say.

"It's you," says Ernest. He eases the coat of feathers from Edith's embrace and hands it to me. She sighs as it leaves her.

"It will be better still when it's finished."

"Maybe," he says. And then, "Don't leave it too long before you come again, Robert."

"No," I promise him, "I won't."

14

You know how bearing grudges is *bad* for you? Does you more damage than the person you're bearing the grudge against? At least that's what the average adult would have you believe? Well, Miss Raynham bears grudges. She's bearing one this morning. Against me. I think it may have something to do with the "or else" situation in the playground on Friday—you know, when I ran and I didn't stop? Today is payback time. So far this bright Monday morning my forgiving homeroom teacher has jabbed chalk in my neck for not knowing the capital city of Ghana (as my English teacher, I'm not sure this is any of her business, but for the record, the answer's Accra and the major languages they speak there are English, Akan, Ga and Ewe); yelled at me for fiddling with my bag (I was only checking on the coat); and scrawled "untidy" over my English homework. I wouldn't have minded the "untidy" (to be honest I did write the poem in rather a rush, under the bedclothes, at about midnight, when I remembered) except that you should see Miss Raynham's writing. It's the sort of mess two drunk spiders might make if they decided to dance on a piece of paper after climbing out of an inkpot. Anyhow, none of this would matter if it wasn't for the moment just before the bell when Miss Raynham says:

"One minute, class. The Mayfield work. Despite my announcement before break that Catherine was in the art room eagerly awaiting all outstanding pieces of work for the triptych, it appears that some of you have still not delivered. I don't think you have to be Einstein to understand that Catherine cannot glue work to a board if she does not have work to glue." Miss Raynham pauses. "Tell me you understand that," and she scans the room, "Robert?"

"Yes, Miss Raynham."

"So you have handed in your work?"

"Erm . . ."

"Would that be a yes or a no, Robert?"

"Erm . . ."

"I'll have to hurry you, Robert."

"Er . . ."

"I'll take that as a no."

"Yes, Miss Raynham."

"Oh. The boy speaks. Now, Robert, is your failure to deliver the work due to your general failure to do anything I ask of you at the moment or is it just bone idleness?"

"Bone idleness, Miss Raynham."

"So it's certainly not that you simply haven't finished the work, Robert?"

"Erm . . ."

"Put simply, Einstein, is your Mayfield work finished or not?"

"Er . . . no," I say. "Not yet."

"Thank you, Robert. Now. Have you any idea why every other child on the project has managed to finish work and you haven't?"

I don't have a reply for that. Not one that would make any sense to Miss Raynham anyway. This gives Niker his opportunity: "Because you can't finish what you haven't started, Miss Raynham."

The class titters.

"I don't remember asking for your opinion, Jonathan Niker," says Miss Raynham swiftly, and I think for a moment that I'm off the hook. But then she turns, with a kind of inevitability, to me and says, "I trust Mr. Niker's assertion is incorrect?"

"Yes! No! I mean . . ."

"You mean?" continues Miss Raynham relentlessly.

"I have started."

"Started?"

"No, not started . . . made . . ."

"Made? What exactly have you made, Robert?"

"Erm . . ."

"Robert!"

"Something."

"Something," Miss Raynham repeats. "You have made something."

"Robert's Elder's been ill," says Kate.

"Yes," says Miss Raynham. "I should think she has. Well, Robert, perhaps you'd like to take the little something you've made down to the art room. And, Robert, may I suggest you do it *right now!*"

The bell goes.

I pick up my bag. I only have one option—to throw myself on Catherine's mercy. Catherine's a storyteller, she will understand, she will know, won't she, that the coat of feathers cannot be glued to a piece of ply-board?

"I said, are you all right?"

"What?" It's Kate asking. "Yes. I'm fine."

"Wesley says something's going on."

"Does he?"

"Says Niker hasn't been the same since you two went to Chance House."

"Oh? He seems much the same to me."

"And he says that you haven't been the same either."

"Leave me alone, Kate." I'm astonished to hear this remark come out of my mouth. It's not so very long ago that if Kate had merely glanced in my direction I could have lived off the experience for a week. And if, in that same not so very long ago, she had come this close and breathed this concern about me, I might have burst from joy. So maybe I have changed. Maybe I am just exhausted. Yes, I think that could be it. Now I think about it, my legs are poles of lead. As I clank my way to the art room, I want to shut my eyes. To sleep. But there's no chance of that. My restless brain is stitching my eyelids open.

The art room door is ajar. I brace myself before pushing it wide. But the room is empty. At the far end, the tables have been moved to make room for Catherine's panels. There are six panels, each only slightly smaller than a door. They lie on the floor in two hinged groups of three. I haven't thought at all about the work the others have been making and am drawn immediately by the form and color of the first triptych. Three-quarters complete, it's a paradise garden with Albert's path walking through it. The garden is made of leaf prints, hand prints and drawings of birds: sparrows, robins, a parrot, Mavis as an angel chicken. Written on Albert's paving stones are fragments of song, memories, statements about the future. "When I am eighty," it says in Weasel's writing, "I will still support Manchester United Football Club." One stone says in wobbly old-person's writing: "I didn't deserve this life," underneath which someone else has graffitied, "Yes, you did."

The second screen is much less finished. There are large white gaps where work should be. The color of it is also quite different. Instead of the browns and greens of earth and garden, this triptych is the color of fairy tales, gold and silver and electric blue. On the left-hand panel is a picture of a prince with a gloved hand over his mouth. It's obviously the Silent Prince and the work is Niker's. The Prince has that exact and haunting beauty that all Niker's drawings have.

Around the Prince is a crowd of lesser people, their gifts of wisdom speech-bubbled over their heads: "Little piggies have big ears, that's what"; "If you can't do a good turn, don't do a bad one." A painted parchment scroll flows like the path in the other triptych to join all three panels together. On the left-hand panel, someone, Catherine presumably, has written in copperplate: "The King and Queen had all but given up their quest to make the young Prince speak when, from the woods nearby, came one last adventurer. This young girl, having consulted her grandparents, told the Prince this story. . . ."

On the central panel, in the same copperplate hand, the young girl's story is written. It is the Firebird story, and it is told, almost word for word, as Edith Sorrel told it. And as if this were not enough, above the story is a white gap the exact shape and size of the coat of feathers. It could not be more accurate if the coat were a jigsaw piece and this the puzzle from which it had been cut. My heart begins tom-tomming, just as it did when I ascended the steps to the top floor of Chance House. Part of me wants to lay the coat in this space, tom, tom, tom, part of me doesn't. All of me wants to read on.

"I have a question," the young girl says on the central panel. "Now that the woman has found her coat of feathers again, what should she do?"

"Then the Silent Prince opened his mouth and he spoke."

And there the story stops. The scroll on the third panel is blank.

"Robert."

"Catherine!" I wheel around, but it is not Catherine. It is Kate.

"What happens?" I yell.

"I'm sorry?"

"In the story, Kate. What happens in the story? Does she go, does she fly away? Does she leave the boy?"

"What are you talking about, Robert?"

"The Firebird story, Kate! The Firebird story, what happens?"

Kate has now arrived beside me. She looks down at what's written. "That's it. That's as far as Catherine told it."

"Catherine told it?"

"Yes, the last time we were at the home. You know she did. You were there."

"I wasn't there. I was with Mrs. Sorrel. And she told it, too. The same story. Exactly, exactly the same!"

"Oh—right."

"And Mrs. Sorrel stopped in the same place. Didn't go on, didn't finish the story, didn't say what happens in the end."

"I'm not sure the ending matters, does it? I mean isn't the point that the girl gets the Prince to speak?"

"No. No! That's not the point at all!"

"Oh—so what is the point?"

"The point is . . . is she going to die?"

"What?"

"Is she going to die?"

"Who? What are you talking about? It's not even a story about dying."

"It's not even a story."

"OK. It's not even a story. In fact it's not a story. It's a flowerpot."

"This isn't a joke, Kate."

"I never said it was."

"You think I'm mad, don't you?"

"I never said that either."

"Mum said it. Robert is an obsessive. Robert's gone bonkers. Told Dad on the phone, your son is bonkers. But you're a fair-minded sort of person, Kate. You'll need proof. Well, here it is." I pull the Sainsbury's bag out of my backpack, unfold the coat of feathers and lay it in the space above the Firebird story. It fits. Perfectly.

"What on earth . . . oh." Kate crouches down to look. "Where did you get this? It's amazing."

"I made it."

"Made it!" She can't help her hand reaching. She touches one of the pure white feathers, then goes deeper, burying her hand in the darker feathers. "Amazing," she repeats. "It's as though it's, it's . . . it feels . . ."

"Alive," I say.

"Yes. That's it exactly. Like a real bird." She looks up at me. "It's warm!"

"Yes, I know." And I do know, though I've been

trying not to notice. Trying to believe that the warmth is just the weight of feathers. And maybe it is just the weight of feathers, or the layering, or . . . But Kate feels it too. I crouch down beside her and put my hand next to hers. Touch her pale and slender fingers.

"I'm sorry," I say then.

"What for?" She doesn't move her hand.

". . . Stuff."

"Do you want to tell me what all this is about?" She smiles, hope and anxiety mixed, but the dimple comes anyway and of course I want to tell her everything. But I don't have the chance because Niker comes in.

He looks at me, at Kate and at the coat of feathers, and he says: "So that's your game."

The words are simple but the venom is like a snake bite. I jump up, stand in front of the coat of feathers like I am standing guard.

"You've been planning this, haven't you? It's what you were doing in the toilets that day."

"I don't know what you're talking about."

"Oh, yes you do."

"Trust me, Niker, I don't."

"OK. Let me spell it out for you. I'm talking about that putrid pile of chicken muck." He points past me to the coat of feathers.

I snatch up the coat, hold it to my breast. "This has nothing to do with you."

"Glad to hear that, Norbert. Because I've been working long and hard on the Firebird coat. The coat that Catherine specifically asked me to make. The one that the editor of the local rag is interested in photographing, alongside its talented creator. And I am not looking to be upstaged at the last minute by some creep with a bunch of chicken feathers."

"Pigeon," I say. "Seagull."

"Oh, Jonathan, is it finished?" Catherine billows into the room with her long swirling skirts and a huge pot of glue.

"Yes," Niker says. "It is."

"Come on then. Let's see."

From beneath his arm Niker takes a roll of paper, which he unfurls to reveal a vivid painting in red and yellow and gold. It is the suit of golden feathers, the storybook Firebird coat, intricate and fabulous and, to my eyes, totally lifeless.

"Oh my," says Catherine, "that is completely wonderful. Look at the color!"

"Thank you," says Niker. "Thank you, fans." He takes a bow.

"What happens next?" I ask Catherine.

"Next? I stick it to the board, I suppose." Catherine waves the glue jovially.

"No. In the Firebird story. What happens"—I point to the third and final panel—"there?"

"A good Scheherazade keeps the customers guessing." Catherine taps the side of her nose. "All will be revealed at the Sharing."

"No," I say. "You don't understand. I need to know. Now. Does the woman fly away? Does she leave the boy?"

"Questions, questions." Catherine smiles.

"Tell me!" I yell.

Catherine puts down the glue pot. "A story," she says, "may end many ways."

"But how does this one end?"

"Depends who's telling it," she says. And, when she sees me about to protest, she adds seriously, "You need to listen to the storyteller as well as the story."

"I don't understand."

"This story comes from the Cree, from the Iroquois. But also from the lips of everyone who's ever told it and the ears of those who have heard." She looks at me strangely. "Who's telling your story, Robert?"

"Mrs. Sorrel."

"Well, then."

"You mean I have to ask her?"

"Would that be such a bad thing?"

"No." I reach for the Sainsbury's bag, begin to fold away the coat of feathers.

"What's that?" Catherine asks.

"Nothing."

"It's a pile of chicken muck," says Niker.

"Let me see," says Catherine.

"No."

"Show her," says Kate.

"No."

"Please," says Catherine, and she comes forward and her hands reach too. So I let her touch. Watch the ripple of the feathers under her fingers.

"Did you make it?"

"Yes. But it's not finished."

"It's quite extraordinary," she says, "It seems . . ."

"Real," says Kate.

"Yes," says Catherine. "Almost." Then she asks me: "Is it part of your story?"

"Yes. Mine and Mrs. Sorrel's."

"Ah—so you're telling the story too?"

"Maybe."

She nods and then returns her attention to the coat. "It's a quite exceptional piece of work. The quality of the stitching, the design, the whole look and feel of it."

"In fact," says Niker, "Robert is a genius."

"Yes," says Catherine, "yes, I think so. Oh, we must include this, don't you think, Jonathan? Two suits of feathers, why not?"

"Because the story only has one," Niker says.

"Ah, but whose story?" says Catherine.

"And it's a gold suit," says Niker. "A suit of *golden* feathers."

"But then you have to ask what's gold," says Catherine. "What's golden? Except brilliant things, excellent things, precious things."

"Right," says Niker. "So I guess that excludes a pile of chicken feathers."

"Come on, Jonathan," says Catherine. "You've got a good eye. Look."

"I'm looking," says Niker. "It's filthy. It smells. It's made of dead things. I don't think it's going to pass Health and Safety. Let alone Matron."

"If it smells of anything," I say, "it will be rose geranium. But don't worry, Niker. I'm not competing. You're welcome to the center panel, center stage and your picture in the paper for all I care. There's no way this coat of feathers is getting stuck down anywhere."

"Hang on a minute," says Catherine. "If you and Mrs. Sorrel have made the work, if it's project work, then—"

"No," I say, pushing the coat too quickly inside the Sainsbury's bag. "Sorry." I can hear the need in my voice and so can Niker.

Unerringly he's on to it—on to me. "Come on, Norbe, quality piece of work like that, work of genius. Should be seen. Am I right or am I right?"

"Sorry," I say. I shouldn't have baited him. Why did I have to say that about center stage, why did I have to let on that the one thing I want least in the world is for the coat of feathers to be stuck down? "I mean, it's not finished yet."

"It's really only the back that needs some attention," says Catherine.

"Yeah," says Niker. "And that doesn't matter, 'cos that's the bit that's gonna get glue on. Right?" He picks up the large pot of paste.

"No!" He's blocking my exit, standing between me and the door. "Kate? Catherine!"

"Leave it, Niker," says Kate.

"What?" says Niker, advancing. "Let Norbert here hide his light under a bushel? Deny the world's media their next Leonardo? Come on, Norbe, hand over the goods."

"I don't think Robert needs to be forced," says Catherine.

"Too right," continues Niker, with menacing glee. "He's gonna share, isn't he? That's what these pieces of work are being made for, aren't they Catherine? For the Sharing." He's brandishing the glue brush. "So I'd say Chicken Muck here is going to share."

It's then that I decide to make a run for it. He's between me and the door so I scramble up on one of the tables, thinking I can get behind him that way. But, quick as a whip, he's up too. He swaggers toward me, grinning from ear to ear. The truth is, he's bigger than me and he's faster than me. But I'm the one with something to lose. I have two choices: track backward until I hit the wall—or jump.

I jump.

A huge pirouette in the air, right over the fairy-tale triptych, to land, with a degree of grace, at Catherine's feet. She lets out a little gasp, and I stop to say "Sorry," which is a mistake. Because anywhere I can jump, Niker can jump too. And he does. Right on top of me. Catherine gasps again. Niker does not say "Sorry," he grabs for the Sainsbury's bag.

"Give it!" he says.

"No way."

"I said *give* it, Feather Boy."

Together we barge into Catherine, who says, quietly and ineffectually, "Stop it, you two. Stop it at once."

Niker's pulling and I'm resisting. The plastic bag rips. And then he has his hand on the coat. He pulls that. He pulls Mrs. Sorrel's coat of feathers. Then I find something. It's anger.

"Don't you dare," I scream.

He laughs. Pulls harder. He hasn't got a proper grip. Or that's what I think, not a grip on the whole coat, just a finger round one of the feathers. One of the white ones, the pure white one I found on the beach. The one I stitched on top of the gray Chance House feather. And I know that my stitches are strong, he cannot dislodge either of my feathers. He cannot. I think one tug may make the coat mine again. I tug. But he's caught the feather below now. Somehow got both hands round it and I hear the snap.

"I'll kill you!" I yell.

He thinks he's got it now, but he hasn't. The quills are resisting him, bent but not broken. So he twists, he twists where the downy part of the flight is, and I should let go, I should just give the coat to him, but I can't and I won't, and so he twists and he twists and the flights break. The white seagull feather and the Chance House feather are both in his hands.

That's when I hit him. You know me well by now and I am not strong and I am not violent but I hit him like I am a rock and he is a piece of rubber. The more he bounces back the more I hit him. I hit his rubber head and his rubber neck and his rubber breast and his rubber arms and I kick his rubber legs. And I keep on hitting and kicking him until he doesn't bounce back anymore. He just lies on the floor. Totally still.

There is blood coming from his nose. Or his forehead. Or maybe it's his eye. Somewhere in the room, someone is crying. It's Kate. There are tears streaming down her face. I look about me. The room is mayhem, chairs upturned, five or six of them all in the wrong places. The steel leg of one has gone through the central panel of the fairy-tale triptych. Someone must have thrown it there. I don't think it can have been me. But, from the look on Catherine's face, maybe it was. She's standing in the doorway with Miss Raynham. Both of them look too shocked to speak.

But Miss Raynham does speak. "Get an ambulance," she says to Catherine. Then she strides across the room and picks me bodily off the floor. "Whatever explanation you have," she says, "it's not going to be good enough."

Then she takes away the coat of feathers.

15

They don't get an ambulance for Niker. Turns out he can stand after all. But he does have to go to Casualty on account of the gash above his right eye. Niker's dad arrives to collect him. His *dad*. At the hospital they clean him up and put on those butterfly sutures they use these days instead of stitches. The nurse who sticks him together is Irene Watson. I know this because Irene Watson is a friend of my mother's. When Niker tells Irene, by way of conversation, that he's been duffed up by a maniac called Robert Nobel, Irene tells my mum. Naturally enough, Mum calls Niker a liar and informs Irene that there is no way her son would hit anyone, least of all a boy like Jonathan Niker. She is in midflow apparently (she has had enough of that Jonathan Niker, is going to go into school and sort out the situation once and for all) when someone finally brings her the message: Your son's school called, they have him in cold storage, perhaps you'd care to go and collect him?

You'd expect her to be angry. I expect her to be angry. What I'm not expecting is what I actually see on her face when she arrives: terror. It is as though some deep part of her believes that, this time, her son really has lost it. It's that look, that fear, that finally puts my brain back inside my body. Up until this moment I've been drifting. Sitting in the room they call the Chiller, a bleak little place next to the headmaster's study, and listening to the talk. And they've all been talking: Mr. Orde, the school social worker; Mr. Blacket, headmaster; Miss Raynham; even Catherine. All of them talking and discussing and being reasonable. And if they've asked me questions, and they have, I've answered them, but only in the way you do when the question isn't really very important. "Regret" and "remorse" are words that have been bandied about. And I think I've been asked if I feel either of these things. But the truth is I've had very little in the way of feelings for the last couple of hours, either for myself or for Niker. But the moment I see my mum's face I want to say sorry.

"Sorry, Mum."

I see some of her fear drain away then. She walks over to where I'm standing alone and puts her arms about me. Then she says, lioness-fierce: "Things haven't been easy for Robert at home. If it's anybody's fault it's mine."

The social worker ahems and then Mr. Blacket starts a speech about how he knows it's a first offense but in the light of the severity of the physical attack, not to mention the damage to school property, they have no option but to suspend me. We will be receiving a letter about how long the suspension will be for, but it is unlikely to be for less than a week. There's some more discussion and Mr. Orde mentions "counseling" more than once. Finally, Mum says: "Robert looks exhausted. May I take him home now?"

It's the middle of the afternoon but she makes me hot milk and puts me to bed. I sleep. When I wake at 8 P.M. she asks me no questions except what I'd like in my sandwiches. Then I sleep again until the morning.

At breakfast, she sits with me, which she doesn't always, and says: "Now would you like to tell me what all this is really about?"

Afterward, I realize she must have been asking me for a different story. But of course there isn't a different story. There's only the truth and when I try to tell it she exclaims: "That wretched coat!" And when I say how that wretched coat could save Mrs. Sorrel's life and how Niker was tearing it, breaking it, and so maybe breaking Mrs. Sorrel's life, all that happens is that the fear comes back into her eyes.

"I'm going to ring your father," she says and puts the phone on speaker.

It's 7:50 A.M. and she gets Dad's new wife on the line. "I need to talk to Nigel," Mum announces. Jo huffs and we can hear the morning commotion as she hands over the phone.

"This is not a convenient time," says Dad.

"It's never a convenient time for you," says Mum. "It wasn't a particularly convenient time for me yesterday afternoon when I was called at the hospital by your son's school and told to collect him because he was being suspended for beating up another child."

"What!" says Dad.

"You heard. And if you want to hear more, perhaps you'd care to make a visit."

"This really isn't fair, Annie. You know perfectly well that the earliest time I can visit is Friday and that's when Robert has his . . . thing."

'Not anymore he doesn't," says Mum. "No school. No Sharing. So Friday will be a fine time. See you then." She puts down the phone.

"What!" I say.

"He's coming Friday."

"But the Sharing! No one's said anything about me being suspended from the Sharing."

"Since the flashpoint for the fight, as I understand it," says Mum grimly, "was work for the Sharing, I hardly think they're going to invite you back to run amok in the home, do you?"

"But I have to be there!"

"Sorry, Robert. No."

"But they haven't said anything about the Sharing. No one's mentioned it!"

"Well, I'm mentioning it. You're not only suspended, you are grounded, young man. So even if they do say you can go, I say you can't. *Finito.* End of story. Right now it's more important for you to see your dad."

"Not to me, it isn't. Not to Mrs. Sorrel!"

"Robert, look at me."

I look at her.

"In less than five minutes I have to leave for work. If I don't leave, and I've thought about not leaving, then I will probably lose my job as well as my mind. If I lose my job, neither of us will be able to eat. So you have to promise me, Robert, not to leave the house. Not to go anywhere near the school. Not to go near the home. In short, not to go out, Robert. Do you understand me?"

"I understand you."

"So promise."

"I . . ."

"Do it."

"I promise not to go . . . near the school."

"Robert?"

"Yes, yes, I said it, didn't I?"

She puts on her coat. "You've got your work sheets, haven't you?"

"Yes. Ten pages of math. Can't wait."

"Well, I want to see all of it done by the time I get back."

"What time will you be back?"

"What do you take me for? A fool? I could be back anytime," she announces. "Bye now. And Robert?"

"Yes?"

"I love you."

"Yes, Mum."

I watch her go. I'm not such a fool either. Most of her shifts are eight hours, and the journey to the hospital adds at least three quarters of an hour each way, longer if she's returning home between four and five. So I reckon I have plenty of time, which is good, because I need plenty of time. I have to get into school and find the coat. I have to retrieve the two feathers Niker broke and get more feathers from the graveyard and the beach. And, most important of all, I have to get to Mrs. Sorrel. Check that she's all right. I promised Ernest. "Don't leave it too long before you come again," he said. And I said: "I promise." Surely this promise, made first, takes precedence over the promise I made Mum? Especially as I also promised Mrs. Sorrel I'd make the coat. And in any case, a promise to save someone's life has to be more important than a promise to abide by some rule and regulation made up by a school. Doesn't it? Doesn't it!

So how come every time I try to put my jacket on I hesitate? It's 8:15 and I'm still dithering by the front door, jacket half on, half off, when the bell rings. It makes me jump. Mum says I should never open the door without looking through the spyhole first. I open the door without looking through the spyhole. It's Kate.

"Hi," she says.

"Hello."

"Can I come in?"

I am not allowed into the outside world, but no one has said anything about the outside world coming into my home. "Sure," I say, and stand aside. Kate Barber, she of the irresistible dimple, walks into my hall.

"I was just on my way to school," she says (which as we know from the relative geography of her house and mine cannot be true), "and I thought I'd stop by. To see how you are."

"To see how I am?" I motion the angel into the kitchen. She sits down at the kitchen table. "I'm fine."

Anyone would be fine whose dimpled angel had finally consented to come into their house and sit at their kitchen table.

She raises an eyebrow.

"I've been suspended," I add.

"Yes, I heard."

There's a pause.

"How's Niker?" I ask.

"I went to see him last night."

"Oh?" A surge of disappointment. She visited him too. And first.

"He's OK. Physically all right, that is. But I think he's quite shocked."

There's a silence. Then I ask the thing that's been troubling me. "Why didn't he hit me back?"

"He did." She looks at me curiously. "Or tried to. Don't you remember?"

"Not exactly." And I don't remember exactly. The events of the afternoon have congealed into a red blur.

"He just couldn't connect. You were too strong for him."

"Too strong for Niker?"

"Yes. You got bigger. Right in front of my eyes. You grew."

"That's what Mrs. Sorrel said. She said I'd got bigger. But I think she meant inside."

"But it *was* sort of inside. As though there was something or someone inside you doing the fighting.

221

A Hercules. A superman. Whatever Niker did, he couldn't have won. It was as if you had the moral right of the whole world on your side."

"Hitting people is wrong," I mention.

"Oh, I know. And it was horrible too. Seeing you pound him like that. And part of me kept thinking, it's not his fault, leave him alone. . . ." She trails off and then she pulls something from her bag. "Here, I brought you something."

It is the coat of feathers.

"Oh, thank you, Kate. Thank you, thank you, thank you." I gather the coat to me. "You don't know what this means to me."

"Yes, I do," she says. "That's it really, that's what I saw yesterday. This isn't just a piece of art or a bunch of feathers, is it? It's something else. Something bigger."

"Yes," I say.

"Can you tell me?"

"It's . . . it's Mrs. Sorrel's life," I say. Kate doesn't laugh. "That's what I was fighting for. Her life." Kate's face does not fill with fear. I tell her everything. Pour it out, overwhelmed with gratitude to be able to talk to someone who is prepared to listen. "So you see," I conclude, "I have to finish the coat and I have to go to the Sharing."

She nods.

"How did you get the coat anyway?" I ask.

"Told Miss Raynham that Catherine needed it, that she'd asked me to fetch it."

"I don't know how to thank you."

"You already have. Now—what else can I do?"

"I need more feathers. From the graveyard. Pigeon feathers. Or from the beach. As many as you can. I have to finish the coat quickly. And I also need those feathers Niker broke. At least the gray one. The Chance House feather. That triggered Mrs. Sorrel, that started her desire for the coat. I need that feather back, Kate."

Again she nods. Then she says: "Robert?"

"Yes?"

"What really happened to Niker in Chance House?"

"Nothing." His being scared doesn't seem so important anymore.

"OK," she persists, "what happened to you, then? What changed you?"

I shrug.

"It's like you found something there."

"I did."

"What?"

"The feather. Three feathers actually."

"Seriously, Robert."

"Seriously, Kate. Three feathers and . . . some

confidence maybe." I look at her angel face. "Courage even. And do you know what? I sometimes think that's exactly what Mrs. Sorrel sent me there to find. So you see, I reserve my right to remain a tiny bit bonkers after all."

"I like you bonkers," Kate says, and smiles. And this time the dimple is especially and only for me. And I am at last my own dream, a boy standing on the edge of a lake throwing stones and watching as the water radiates dimples. "I'll find that Chance House feather for you," Kate continues, "and the white one."

"They may just be on the art room floor," I say. "Or chucked in the bin."

"I'll check. And I'll ask Niker. And after school I'll go to the beach and the graveyard. I'll get those feathers. As many as you need."

"Thank you. Thank you forever."

"I have to go now. But I'll be back. You'll see."

When she goes a light seems to go out of the house. I fret. I want to visit Mrs. Sorrel now, immediately. But I have to be careful and I have to be wise. The most important thing is to finish the coat and now, with Kate's help, I can do that without leaving the house. If I'm caught away from home now, Mum's tenuous trust in me will be broken. And my only hope of getting to the Sharing is if Mum still has confidence in me, believes that I'll stay put. Otherwise *she'll* stay put. Sit in the house with me.

But what's to stop me phoning? Making contact that way? Mayfield has one of those wheelie phones they have in hospitals. I've seen it. They can just wheel it to Mrs. Sorrel's bed and then I'll tell her everything. I'll tell her to hang on, that the coat is coming, that everything will be all right.

I get the number from the phone book. I call and the phone is picked up straightaway. It's Matron. I'd recognize her voice anywhere. Heart pounding, I slam the phone down. I should have thought of that. I should have had a plan. So I do some thinking, try my luck again. This time it isn't Matron.

"Good morning," I say. "Is it possible to speak to Edith Sorrel?"

There's a pause.

"Who's calling?"

"Her nephew. Ian."

"Ian?" the voice queries.

"Ian Wright," I say quickly. Ian Wright! The retired soccer star of Arsenal and West Ham? Where did he come from? I hold my breath but the care assistant seems oblivious.

"Could you hang on a minute?" she says. "I'll get Matron for you."

Pound, pound, pound. That's the heart again. Should I put the phone down? Ian Wright wouldn't do that. A courageous boy wouldn't do that. I hang on, as instructed.

"Mr. Wright?" Matron's voice.

"Yes," I say gruffly.

"I take it you are aware of Mrs. Sorrel's condition?"

"Yes." Same gruff stuff. "I thought, as, um, I'm unable to visit right now, I might be able to speak to her by phone?"

"I'm afraid that won't be possible. The news is not good, Mr. Wright."

My heart skips a beat.

"Yesterday lunchtime, your aunt slipped . . . into a coma. Of course, things could change, but at the moment I have to tell you her doctor believes the prognosis is not good." There is a pause, which I am unable to fill. "Would you care to leave a message for Mr. Sorrel?"

"No. Yes. Tell him . . . tell him . . . the boy who can fly keeps his promises."

"I beg your pardon?" says Matron.

16

Kate is as good as her word. She brings me a pocketful of feathers, gray, white, clean, downy, dry. Dry! They can all be sewn immediately.

"Are there enough?" she asks.

"No, I don't think so. But I'm really grateful any-how."

"I'll bring you more. I'll go again tomorrow."

"What about the Chance House feather, did you get that?"

"No. I tried. Scoured the art room. The bin hadn't been emptied so if it had been chucked I would have found it. But it wasn't there. Nor on the floor. I did every inch of it. And I asked Catherine. She denied all knowledge."

"And Niker?"

"'What would I want with some filthy feather?'" she mimics.

"Did you believe him?"

She hesitates. "I don't know. But I can't see any reason why he would keep it."

"Trophy. Going-home present."

"He was flat on his back, Robert. Probably wasn't the first thing on his mind."

"And because it must have been obvious to him how important the feather is to me."

"But is it important to the coat? I mean, if you finish the coat, isn't that good enough?"

"Yes. Maybe."

"What's the 'but'?"

She's acute, that Kate. Because, of course, there is a "but." The one I've been trying to keep secret even from myself.

"Come on," she says.

Things that exist only in your head can be kept vague, pushed away, but once something is spoken aloud . . .

"Tell me," she says, and takes my hand. Kate takes my hand.

"I called the home. Spoke to Matron."

"Yes?"

"Mrs. Sorrel's gone into a coma."

"Oh, my goodness."

"And . . . and guess when she took this dive?"

"Oh, I don't know, Robert. Don't give me a quiz on this."

"Yesterday lunchtime. Not the morning. Not the evening. Not the day before. But yesterday lunchtime. When Niker and I were fighting. When the feather was broken."

I see a shiver travel down Kate's spine. "Could be a coincidence," she says.

"Yes," I say. "Could be."

Out in the hall, a key turns in the lock. Kate jumps up and her hand goes with her. I shove the feathers behind a cushion.

"Oh—hello, Kate!" says Mum.

"Hello, Mrs. Nobel."

"To what do we owe the pleasure?"

"Miss Raynham," flusters Kate. "She asked me to drop something by for Robert. You don't mind, do you?"

"Work?" inquires Mum.

"Work. Yes," says Kate.

"No, I don't mind."

"Kate was just leaving," I say.

"Well, don't hurry on my account."

Kate hurries. She's out of the door in a flash. "I'll bring Miss Raynham's . . . erm . . . other stuff tomorrow," she calls over her shoulder.

Mum regards me but says nothing. She kicks off her shoes.

"Good day?" she inquires at last.

"OK," I reply.

"Get your math done?"

"Some."

"Well, there's good news on the work front."

"Yes?"

"I've got tomorrow off."

"What?"

"And the day after."

"Why!"

"I do get days off, Robert. Code of working practice in the National Health Service. Good behavior. Whatever."

She's taken a vacation! I stay in, good as gold all day, and she takes time off. It's not fair!

"So I'll be able to keep you company."

"Nice," I say.

"The less good news is I'll have to work Friday evening. But I think time alone with your dad will be no bad thing, don't you?" I say nothing. "Good," she says. "That's settled then."

Well, it certainly settles what I'm going to have to do about Niker.

"Mum?"

"Yes?"

"Do you think I could borrow the phone? Take it up to my room?"

"Can I ask why?"

"I want to call Niker. Apologize."

"Oh, Robert."

"But . . . I sort of want to do it in private. You know . . . because . . ."

"You're a good boy really." She kisses the top of my head.

I take the phone and, when she's not looking, the feathers from under the cushion, and go to my room. Of course I'd rather go to Niker's house, look him in the eye when I ask the question, but obviously with Mum at home that's not going to be possible. And some things won't wait.

I dial the number.

"Hello?"

"Hello, Mrs. Niker, it's Robert Nobel here."

"Oh."

"May I speak to Johnny?"

"I'm not entirely sure he will wish to speak with you."

"Please, Mrs. Niker."

A pause.

"Could you just ask him? I want to apologize. Say sorry."

"Oh." Her tone softens. "All right then. I'll ask." She puts her hand over the receiver and I hear some mumbling. Then Niker comes on the line.

"Hiya, Dog-Brain."

"Hello, Niker."

Silence.

"I gather you've got something to say to me?"

"Sorry," I say.

"You will be," he replies. "Trust me."

"Niker?" I have to keep my temper.

"Yes, Norbert?"

"Niker—do you remember when we were in Chance House?"

"I have some vague recollection."

"And you liked me?"

"What!"

"You liked me. Niker. Just a little bit? Maybe?"

"No. That doesn't compute."

"You thought I was funny."

"That computes."

"And I thought you were nice. I liked you, Niker."

Another silence, but a more interested one.

"Well," I forge on, "I am really sorry about what happened in the art room. I shouldn't have hit you. It was all wrong. Hitting people is wrong."

"Yeah, yeah."

"But . . ."

"Oh, here we go."

"But it was about Mrs. Sorrel."

"It was?"

"Now, I don't expect you to understand this, because it barely makes any sense to me, but you have to trust me, because I'm going to trust you. OK?"

"Which planet are we on now, Norbert?"

"The coat of feathers isn't just a coat of feathers."

"Right you are, Norbe."

"It's connected to Mrs. Sorrel's life. You know she's been ill?"

"I know she's been ill."

"Well, when we fought, when that feather, the gray one I found at Chance House, when that got broken, Mrs. Sorrel got worse. Much worse, Niker. Dyingly worse, Niker."

"Oh—*that* planet."

"So I need the feather back. And the white one if you've got it. I have to have them. Sew them on the coat."

"And what if I haven't got them?"

"Have you got them, Niker?"

A pause.

"Niker!"

"No. Sorry. Not at home. Goodbye." He puts the phone down.

"Niker!" I scream. All niceness, all cooperation, all apology vanishes. I want to kill him. I'm going to go round to his house and kill him. Now.

"He didn't accept the apology?" Mum, hearing me scream, has come upstairs.

"Yes. No!"

Mum sits on my bed. "Sometimes it's as difficult to accept an apology," she says, "as it is to offer one. But well done for trying."

"Right."

"Do you want to play cards?"

"What?"

"Cards. Cribbage. Sevens."

"Where have cards come from?" I look at her face. "Is this some brainwave from Mr. Jolly Kind Counseling, social worker?"

She havers. "No."

Me lying to Mum, I've tried not to think too much about that recently. But her lying to me—that's painful.

"I just thought," Mum continues, "perhaps we don't play as much as we used to."

"Mum," I say in as grown-up a voice as I can manage, "none of this is your fault."

"I wish your dad was here," she says.

"I know."

And so begins the dance we do round each other for the next few days. I try really hard at being normal.

Norbert Normal. I've almost forgotten what it's like. I eat with Mum, talk with her, even play cards. I'm quite good at cribbage actually. Then I live my secret life. I spend a lot of it hating Niker. I believe he has the Chance House feather, and probably the white one too. I imagine climbing out of my bedroom window when Mum's asleep, going round to his house, shinning up a drainpipe and (as I've never been to his house and therefore don't know which room is his) dropping into his parents' bedroom by mistake. "Oh— hi, Mrs. Niker, didn't wake you, did I?" Because this scenario doesn't seem to "compute," to use Niker's word, I manufacture a second one. In this one Niker invites me round for a face-to-face reconciliation. I tell Mum I have to be there at a certain time and no matter what time I make it, Mum always says: "Fine. I'll come with you." So that just leaves me making a break for it in broad daylight and commandeering an armored tank. But I still might not be able to find the feather. Where would a person like Niker hide it anyway?

"What are you thinking, Robert?"

"I'm thinking about having a bath."

I'm taking lots of baths. About four times as many as usual. Mum has remarked upon my cleanliness. She's worried that washing might be becoming my new obsession. I can't tell her that actually it's the old obsession. Sewing. I conceal the coat and Kate's feathers inside my bathrobe, run a bath and sew behind the locked bathroom door. After an hour or so I actually get into the bath, which by then, of course, is cold. They say that cold water sharpens your brain. It doesn't seem to sharpen mine. My plans still go in circles and nothing stops me from worrying about Mrs. Sorrel.

During the two days Mum only leaves the house once—to get eggs. That's when Ian Wright rings the home again to inquire about Edith Sorrel's condition. The care assistant tells him that his aunt's condition is no better but no worse either. I take this as good news, what I would expect. No more broken feathers, so not worse. No completed coat, so not better. On the pretext of science homework, Kate arrives with more feathers. She even manages to get some of the very tiny, downy white ones I wanted for the breast. I sew. And I sew.

On Friday the coat is finished.

"Don't forget," Mum says, "Dad will be here at seven. Look through the spyhole. Don't let anyone else in."

"Yes, Mum."

But at seven, of course, I'm not there to let anyone in. I leave the house at 6:20 P.M. Five minutes after Mum. It is the first time I have been outside for four days. The air smells different. Springlike. The trees are green-budded and even the apple tree in the Dog Leg is covered with pink blossom. And although it's dusky, it's still light. All good omens.

I begin my journey full of purpose and hope. The coat, folded in its plastic bag, is heavy. I carry it close to my breast, one hand outside, around the bag, and the other inside, buried deep among the feathers. Its warmth is palpable. My living, breathing coat. Once, I imagine I even feel a heart beating there. But of course it is only my heart I feel through the feathers. The beat, beat, beat of my brisk walk toward Mrs. Sorrel.

I arrive at Mayfield at five to seven and slip around the back of the home. There is a little crack of light coming from the fire door. Kate's doing. Kate's promise to me. "Of course I'll get there early, open the door for you." I am quickly through into the hallway. It's now the shortest of walks along the corridor to Edith's room. But I have forgotten to take account of the residents' lounge opposite. Tonight its double doors are flung wide and there is a buzz of activity inside. I flatten myself against the wall, as though keeping still will render me invisible. What if Matron is there?

Immobilized, I stare. The room has been rearranged. The chairs that normally line the walls have been moved into graceful audience half-moons. Some of the residents, unable to identify their normal places, haver and mill. At the stage end of the room, Catherine throws a sheet over the paradise-garden triptych. The Firebird screen stands unveiled to her left. Even from this distance, Niker's fabulous coat of golden feathers draws the eye. Standing either side of the coat are Niker and Mavis the chicken. Niker, at twelve, the taller of the two. On his knees before them, shooting upward, is a photographer.

"Heads a bit closer," he calls. "Mavis, is her name Mavis? Bit closer in, Mavis love."

Mavis doesn't move.

"Is she deaf?" asks the photographer.

"Yes," says Niker.

"Mavis love," the photographer screams, "could you move in a little, love?"

"It'll all come to no good," says Mavis solemnly. "Mark my words."

"Mavis," says Niker, and lifts an arm, motioning her toward him, as if he would embrace her.

She moves in and he does put his arm around her. The sight is so strange and tender that for a moment I don't see the panel that Mavis's movement reveals. It is the third panel. The end of the story. It comes to me slowly across that divide. A frail but beautiful bird flying up into an arcing sky. The arc is a rainbow, brilliant sun but also a shower of rain. Least it should be rain, but there is a boy there crying. And the rain is his tears.

Niker grins. The photographer clicks. Grin, grin, grin. Click, click, click.

"Could that be enough now?" Catherine is hovering with a second sheet.

"Are you the artist?" the photographer asks.

"No," says Catherine, "now if you'll excuse me." She throws the sheet over the Firebird triptych.

Only when the piece is covered does my body unlock. I'm swiftly along the corridor and into Edith's room. By contrast with the residents' lounge, Edith's bedroom is graveyard quiet. There is no movement here at all. Just a tableau in the center of the room. The bed. Edith. Ernest. It's difficult to know which is the stillest: the iron bedstead, the barely breathing Edith, or Ernest, frozen in a posture of utter dejection. I have a long moment to take in the scene before Ernest finally lifts his head. When he sees who it is, he says: "Robert." And then: "Thank God."

I go at once to the bed. "Mrs. Sorrel, it's me. Robert. I'm here."

No response.

"I've finished the coat. It's finished."

No response.

"Mrs. Sorrel." I pull the coat from the bag. "Feel this!"

No response.

I look at Ernest. He shakes his head.

Edith's breathing is shallow but noisy. I've heard Mum speak about this. It's the breathing people do when they are close to death. Nurses call it the death rattle.

"Mrs. Sorrel!" I scream, and I take her limp, white hand and I plunge it into the coat of feathers.

"Ah—ha," she says.

Ernest seems to wake up then.

"Edith?" he says.

We both see her hand move, just the slightest push deeper into the feathers.

"Aaah." Another, longer sigh.

"Do you want it on?" I say. "Do you want to put the coat on?"

She makes another noise, and although it does not sound at all like "Yes," both of us know what her answer is.

I unbutton the pearls.

"I'll lift her," says Ernest. "Edith, Edith darling, I'm going to lift you now. And Robert's going to help you with the coat."

He puts his arm under her neck and around her birdlike shoulders, then very gently he lifts her to an upright position. Her head lolls and she still doesn't open her eyes. But I work to get the coat on. I hold her hand and guide it through the sleeve, I pass the back of the coat around her thin nightdressed shoulders. Ernest maneuvers his hands, never once letting her slip from his embrace. Then I go around to Ernest's side of the bed and help with the second sleeve. Edith sighs as Ernest lowers her onto the bed again. But it is a more contented sigh. I do up the buttons then, my fingers fumbling. I touch the skin of her neck.

"Sorry," I say.

"Love . . . ," she replies.

Ernest gasps. "Edith? Edith, we're here. Robert and I are here. You're all right."

"Yes . . . ," she says, and opens faraway eyes. "Yes."

For a moment she stares at the ceiling and then, painfully slowly, she moves her head first toward Ernest and then toward me. "Hold me," she says. I take her left hand and Ernest her right. Her skin is dry and paper thin but oh—so warm.

"I'm going . . . ," she begins then.

"No," says Ernest. "No, no, no, no, no."

"I'm going . . . ," she repeats, and then smiles a sweet, surprised, angelic smile, "to sing."

Ernest looks stunned. Terrified even. She opens her mouth, clears her dry throat. Then she begins. Makes a painful, rasping noise, the hoarse cough of an instrument on which dust has lain for decades. She shuts her mouth, licks her lips and begins again. A gasp, a croak and then a warble, tremorous, sad and old. She grits her teeth and begins again. And again.

Ernest listens, his face contorted with grief. Even I want to stop her, because she seems to be straining for something so impossibly long gone. And I fear she will burst with the pain of it. But we both just sit and hold her hand as asked until a different sound comes.

And I do not know, even now, where that sound came from. The forlorn stuttering of an old woman giving way to a single note—and then a run of notes—so beautiful it would make you cry to hear them. Pure, clear notes coming not from a dry throat but from a soul in joyous flight. And Ernest is crying. There are tears pouring down his cheeks but he looks, for the first time I've known him, happy.

Then the notes stop. Edith takes a breath and Ernest holds his, and then she begins one final note. Holding her one-note song in a smile that she bestows on Ernest so that they seem, hand-joined there on the other side of the bed, a couple. On my side of the bed, on my hand, I feel the faintest of touches. I can't call it a squeeze, though I want it to be a squeeze, I want it to be her holding me. But she hasn't the energy now. I don't think she can turn her head even. And yet still the note sustains, though fainter now. And fainter. Until it ceases. A last outbreath, and we both wait for her to breathe in again. But she does not.

"Edith!" Ernest's head drops onto his wife's breast. He buries his face in the feathers. "Edith."

And I know that the bird is dead.

My Firebird is dead.

I let go her hand, feeling each of her fingers fall away from mine. Then I stand up. The bedroom door is open though I never heard the latch. Niker is in the doorway. If he opens his mouth, if he says a single word, I will kill him. But he says nothing. Just swallows, and I know he's heard. He must have come because of the song. Niker.

I walk past him into the hall. He doesn't follow me, for which I'm glad. I don't know where I'm going. There doesn't seem any place for me to be now. I'm just walking, wandering. I wander to the open mouth of the residents' lounge. Pausing there only because it's somewhere to lean. To rest my body. Catherine is speaking. She's telling a story. The words float toward me.

"And what happened to the little boy?" asked the Silent Prince.

"Some say," replied the adventurer, "that he cried so long and so hard for his Firebird mother that he lost his voice and became silent. Others say that when he awoke the following morning he found two golden feathers shining on his pillow, and these feathers brought him courage and love and luck for all of his life."

Someone is walking through the words. A man appearing from the edge of the room. His height and gait look familiar. He stops in front of me. It is my father.

"Hello, son," he says.

My head is at the level of his chest. Arms come about me. He holds me warm and tight. Someone begins to sob. It's me.

17

Two days later, Sunday, I'm standing outside Chance House. It was Kate who tipped me off, saw the notice. Redevelopment work is due to start, apparently, in a week's time. Chance House is going to be a youth and unemployment center. There will be offices, computer facilities, a games room with pool, foosball and Ping-Pong, a canteen selling cheap food. I look up at the Top-Floor Flat. What, I wonder, will they put in David Sorrel's room?

"So," says a voice. "Another goodbye."

I don't have to turn to know who it is. But I turn anyway.

"Hello, Mr. Sorrel." It's the first time I have seen Ernest since the Sharing. I expect him to be bowed but he is not.

"Are you going in?" he asks.

I hadn't been thinking of doing anything of the sort, but one look at his face and I say: "Yes."

We walk around the back together. He's brought a cane, an ebony one with a silver knob. He uses it to steady himself on the tussocky ground. He skirts the bottles and the beer cans and the microwave with barely a glance. Nothing seems to surprise him in fact, and I realize, as he passes into the kitchen, that the territory is quite familiar to him. He crosses the kitchen floor and bends to move the brick.

"It was you!" I exclaim. "You all the time. Moving the brick!"

"And you," he replies. "You moved it too."

He straightens up, holds the door for me. "After you."

I go into the corridor. A faint drip, drip, drip.

"Where does the water come from?" I ask.

"That," he says, "I never managed to understand."

There is morning light in the house, and with Ernest beside me, it seems impossible to imagine that one could be frightened here. He moves with care across the smashed-tile hallway and he pokes the wallpaper on the stairs with the stick, just to be sure where the treads begin and end.

"I always expected squatters to move in," he said. "But they never did."

"How long have you been coming here?" I ask.

"Only since the mesh got pulled off the kitchen, about a year I suppose. On and off."

I look at him and he knows what I'm thinking.

"No, of course I didn't pull it off," he laughs. "That's why I expected squatters."

We ascend the final stairs, passing through the fire door and on, up to the landing. He pauses there, but only for a moment, and then he goes into the room with the million ducks. I follow, keeping behind him as he makes his way to the window. He looks out.

"This is the room it happened in," I say. "Isn't it?"

"Yes," he says with his back to me.

Then I can't not know for any longer. "Why did he do it, Mr. Sorrel? Why did he jump?"

"Jump?" Ernest turns around. "David never jumped."

I stand stupefied. Underneath me the floorboard creaks.

"That's just an old story," he adds, not without kindness. "Houses like this attract stories. Especially houses where there has been tragedy." He pauses. "David died of an asthma attack. He couldn't catch his breath."

"Asthma!"

"Yes. Asthma. Just asthma." My face must be registering disbelief because he continues: "It was different in those days. Preventative drugs were not as they are today. He had an attack, a very severe attack. . . ." he trails off. "There was nothing to be done." Ernest taps the floor with his cane. Tap. Tap. Tap. "Nothing and no one could have saved him."

There's a hint of aggression here, the glitter of the crow. He thinks I'm going to contradict him. When I don't, he says into the silence: "But Edith couldn't accept that. Edith thought if she'd been with him, he wouldn't have died. She thought she could have–should have–saved him."

"She wasn't with him?"

"No. He died here. In this room. Alone."

"I don't understand."

"This flat belonged to Marigold Linley. A friend of Edith's. Edith left David with Marigold when she went for her singing lessons."

"I thought you said you stopped her singing," I whisper.

"I did. Or tried to. More fool me. That's why it was a secret. Why the tutor couldn't come to our house. Why Edith had to go out to his house and David–be left here."

"You bullied her!"

"Bullied?" he repeats. "No . . . no, I don't think so.

Well . . . oh, it's difficult to understand now. But women didn't have careers in those days. They were wives and mothers. That's what I wanted her to be. I couldn't see that her sights were—set somewhere else. That she had a star. She had to follow her star." He's leaning on the stick now, his thin body looking suddenly as if it needs support. "Afterward, when I met the tutor, he said she was very good. He said she had a great talent. A great future."

"But she gave it all up!"

"Yes. After David died, she swore she would never, ever sing again. Not a note. And there was to be no music in our house. Even the sound of other people singing, whistling in the street drove her into a frenzy. She was quite mad," he says meditatively, "for a while."

Sunshine comes in at the broken window, and behind Ernest's head, dust motes dance.

"And then?"

"She pushed it all away. Pushed us away. The singing, David, me—we didn't exist anymore. She lived on some other plane, inhabited a different part of her mind. And she wasn't unhappy. She was all right. So I went along with it. I thought it was her way of healing. So I played along."

"You divorced her," I say harshly, although it's none of my business, although it's not my parents' divorce.

"Yes. Because she asked me for that. She wanted it. The final break with the past. I had to go." He smiles wearily. "But I never left her in my heart. And some deep part of her, I think, I hope, understood that."

"I'm sorry," I say then.

"Why?"

"I thought the coat would cure her. I really believed it."

"I know."

"And it would have done. But I got involved in a fight. One of the feathers got broken. One I got from this room. A Chance House feather. I broke it. And then I couldn't find it and that's why she died."

"No," cries Ernest, "don't you dare say that! You must never say, never even think such a thing again." He shakes the stick at me as if it were a fist. "It was not your fault. Edith died of cancer. It happens. People die and it's nobody's fault. That's what Edith refused to accept. For thirty years she blamed herself. Because she wasn't there. Hadn't saved David. But that was rubbish. All the doctors told her so. Nothing and no one could have saved him. But she let her guilt dominate her life. Her music, her talent, her energy, the love we shared, all of it got buried with David.

"And David himself. The son we had both adored.

She couldn't even say his name. Until she met you, Robert. All those years and I wanted so much to talk of him. My boy. My son. If it was anyone's fault it was mine. Not that she didn't blame me. And rightly so. That's why I took everything, the silence, the pushing away, the divorce. I deserved it all. But don't you dare blame yourself, Robert Nobel. You gave Edith everything."

"That night at the Sharing then," I say slowly, "it was the first time . . ."

"Yes. The first time she'd sung. For thirty years. That's what you gave her, Robert. You gave her back her singing. Her song. Returned it to her. Returned her to herself." He draws a deep breath. "And you returned her to me." Then he adds, stiffly, "For which I will never be able to repay you."

"It wasn't all one way," I say then.

"What?"

"She gave me stuff too."

"Yes?"

"She is—was—the first person who ever made me think if I wanted something, I could go for it."

"I wish she could hear you say that. I think that would make her the proudest woman on earth. That opportunity is all she ever really wanted for herself, for David."

" 'You're the sort of boy who can fly,' " I say.

"Yes," he says. "She was always saying that to David. 'You can do it. You can fly. Whatever you want, David, you can make it happen.'" He sighs. "And I should have let her fly. That's what love is. Letting your loved ones fly."

He moves away from the window. "Will you come to the funeral?"

"Yes. Of course."

"Thank you. She would have liked that." He pauses. "I wish I could give you something . . . something of hers . . ."

"Why?" I say. "When she's given me so much?"

"Thank you," he says, all choked up for a moment. "Thank you." Then he recovers himself, tap, tap, taps with the stick. "Well, perhaps we could meet sometimes. Have tea maybe? Or hot chocolate. What would you say to a hot chocolate, Robert?"

"Good morning, hot chocolate."

"I'm sorry?" says Ernest.

"It's one of my dad's jokes. Not brilliant, I admit. But he does have other qualities. Oh." I look at my watch. "I almost forgot. I should be leaving. I'm meeting him for lunch today."

"Another time then."

"Yes."

We leave Chance House together. I say a silent

goodbye to the million mother ducks and the three million ducklings. Ernest taps his way downstairs and out into the spring. As we come round the side of the house, a man with a clipboard shouts: "Oi–this is private! Private property!"

18

And so. The end of my story. I'd like to tell you that my parents got back together again and we all lived happily ever after. That didn't happen. At least the bit about my parents getting back together again didn't happen. Mainly on account of Dad being married to Jo. But I do see him more often now. We go fishing. You can laugh if you like. Plenty of other people have. But I'm good at fishing. Dad says I have nimble fingers. We go to Shoreham beach and fish from the rocks. Depending on the time of year, we might catch flounders, plaice, dabs, codling or whiting. If we need a hook on the line, or a new lure, Dad gives them to me to tie. I can do them faster than he can. All that experience with needles and knots and feathers, you see. The first time he saw me moistening the nylon to get the knot secure he said: "Who taught you that trick?"

I just shrugged. He never asked me about the sewing. Never really asked why I was crying that night at the Sharing. That's also why fishing is so good for us, we can be together, be companionable, without really having to say much.

"Can you do me a tucked half-blood knot?"

"Yes, Dad."

"Thanks, son."

"What would you say to a sandwich, Robert?"

"Hello, sandwich."

Previously it would have made me furious. I would have thought we were drifting by. But there are some things that don't have to be spoken. Maybe can't be spoken. His love for me. It's quite clear. As clear as Ernest's love for Mrs. Sorrel. And I'm not in the business of pushing Dad away, burying him, blaming him. I want him close by. As much of him as he can give. And he gives what he can, when he can, I know that. And I make it enough. One day, when I know how, I'll tell him how much I love him. But then again, maybe I won't. Maybe he knows already.

As for Ernest, I'd like to say that we keep in touch.

More than that, that we've become close, a grandfather-grandson relationship. But that hasn't happened either. I think Ernest has spent so long inside his own stern prison he finds it difficult to walk free. We meet occasionally, at the graveyard, him with flowers, me with my thoughts, and we nod and smile and he asks how I am and I say "I'm fine." There's a new stone by David's. It has Edith's name on it and her dates and one word: "Reunited." The pigeons sit on this stone and I don't shoo them away. Edith wore the coat of feathers in her coffin, was buried in it. That was Ernest's choice. So I reckon the pigeons have a right. As for the hot chocolate, Ernest never repeated his offer and I've never mentioned it. I'm not at all sure what we'd say to each other over hot chocolate. All I know is that he's glad of me and I'm glad of him.

The papers got hold of the story. There was a journalist there that night at the Sharing, as well as the photographer. Dick Miller. He claimed to have heard Mrs. Sorrel singing. I always wonder whether it wasn't actually Niker who told him about it. Niker who needed to download, to talk about the song because it was so extraordinary and so raw and didn't make any sense. At least to him. In any case, when Miller found out who Mrs. Sorrel was, he dredged up the "tragic boy" story of thirty years ago, then added in Chance House and the new developments there, and then he had a story. His story. A newspaper story. He missed the Firebird connection completely and I didn't tell him, though he asked for an interview.

"Did she think you were her son? Did she think you were David, is that why she sang, after all these years?"

I told him nothing. The paper ran the story anyway. They got David's age wrong and also Ernest's name. They called him Eric. I was glad about that. It made the story what it was—nothing to do with anything. But they did mention how David died of asthma and how he had, all those years ago, attended the school that became my school. Which I didn't know, and maybe it wasn't true, but it gave me an idea. Maybe our school should honor David, the memory of him, what he stood for. I mentioned it first to Mum.

"What a good idea," she said. "You could link it to asthma awareness. Maybe even link it to the national campaign. The David Sorrel Asthma Awareness Day."

I stopped the idea right there. Because of course I didn't want that at all. I wanted what Mrs. Sorrel would have wanted, a Boy Who Can Do Anything Day. And I realized you can't really have days about that, it's something that comes from inside. Something that comes from a touch or a belief or a hope. Something that takes root when you stand up and say no to a boy like Jonathan Niker.

Jonathan Niker. I'd like to say that we became, if

not friends, then respectful of each other. That did happen. Not, finally, because of any action of mine, but because of something he did. The day after Mrs. Sorrel's funeral, there was a knock at my door. I answered it to find Niker and Kate standing on my doorstep.

"Johnny has something for you," said Kate.

As soon as Niker reached for his pocket, I knew what it was. What they were. The feathers. Niker brought them out, the gray and broken Chance House feather and the white one from the beach.

"He did have them," said Kate. "Clenched in his hand when he fell."

Niker extended his hand, palm open, and presented the feathers. "And others say," Niker said, "that when he awoke the following morning he found two golden feathers shining on his pillow, and these feathers brought him courage and love and luck for all of his life."

He said it gently, seriously, and I knew he meant the gift not just for me but also for Mrs. Sorrel. "Thank you," I replied. And then I added, just in case: "It wouldn't have made any difference. She would have died anyway. You know that?"

He nodded.

Later I took the feathers to my room. Love—I am blessed enough in that. Courage—I plan to learn more of. And luck. Luck. If Mrs. Sorrel taught me anything, she taught me that you make your own luck. I put the feathers in a drawer.

And then there's Kate. I expect you want to know what happened between me and that angel with the dimple? Sorry. I can't tell you that. At least not right now, because, well, it's kind of a long story. . . .

Acknowledgments

Stories don't come out of nowhere. This one came from my son Roland, who said one day, "Why don't you write something for my age group?" He was eleven then, twelve by the time we'd finished the book. I read it to him chapter by draft chapter. His criticism was exact and wise. I thank him.

I'm grateful to my ten-to-thirteen-year-old "test" readers: Sam Bull, Natalya Wells, Felix Faber, Clare Liddicoat and Matilda Kay. I sent them the first half of the book and a nervous questionnaire. They responded with intelligence (of course), but also with enthusiasm—which was a gift. Matilda even drew pictures.

I thank my sister Jackie. I'm thirteen years older than she is and I used to tell her stories. Now she tells me stories. She told me about an art project she was doing with the residents of St. Edberg's, Bicester. I was privileged to listen to some of the Elders. I acknowledge their wisdoms. I also thank my great-aunt Dorothy, aged ninety-one. With her great gentleness she told me about memory.

I'm grateful to Dan Yashinsky, whose wonderful book, *The Storyteller at Fault* (Ragweed Press), led me to the Silent Prince and the Firebird stories. Yashinsky retells the stories from the Cree and the Iroquois and I retell them from him. Thus go stories.

I thank my agent, Clare Conville, for her faith, her energy and her openness. They mean a lot to me.

And I thank the chance that led me, one day, to a huge, derelict house in downtown Hove and the powerful feeling that I just had to go in. . . .

About the Author

Nicky Singer has worked in publishing, the arts and television. She is the author of four novels and two works of nonfiction for adults published in the United Kingdom. This is her first book for young people.

Nicky Singer lives with her husband and their three children in Brighton, England.